Repressed Echoes
The Sendaxa Chronicles, Book 1

By

REBECCA HEFNER

Cover Design: The Book Brander
Editor: Megan McKeever
Proofreader: Nay's Notations – Editing and Proofreading Services

Contents

For everyone else who needed a book that was a mash-up of The Last of Us and Fifty First Dates. I can't be the only one who loves steamy post-apocalyptic romances with a little amnesia thrown in...right??

Chapter 1

Sometime in the not-so-distant future...

Dr. Danica Lawson's eyes flew open, darting to each corner of the dim room. The only sounds that marred the silence were her soft, labored pants and the pounding heartbeat that infiltrated her inner eardrums. Touching her tongue to the dry roof of her mouth, she tried to swallow, but her throat failed to bob. A soft whimper escaped her lips, and she placed her palm flat on the bed, attempting to push into a sitting position.

Pain seared her side and she gasped, collapsing on the mattress as her fingers found the wound. A thick bandage covered the tender skin, and she wondered how she'd sustained the injury.

Closing her eyes, she took a moment to center herself.

You can do this, Dani. Try to remember.

Cobwebs clouded her brain, obstructing any semblance of rational thought. Her pupils roved under closed lids, searching the darkness for a trace of where she was...how she'd been injured...and how she'd ended up in a strange bed in a dark room.

Obscure shadows were her only answer, and she struggled with the realization she needed to *run*. Lifting her lids, she hastily scanned the room. Whoever had placed her here wasn't present, but they could return any moment.

Now was the time to break free.

Sucking in a breath, she palmed her side, holding the bandage tight, and maneuvered into a sitting position. Glancing down, she noticed the thin shorts and tank top that covered her frame. Black sneakers sat at the foot of the nearby nightstand, and she grabbed them, tugging them on under the small shaft of light that filtered through the curtains of the lone window in the room. Once the shoes were tied, she gradually rose to her feet, placing a hand on her head as the room began to spin.

"Come on, Dani," she whispered, lowering her hand and straightening her spine. "Let's go."

Gritting her teeth, she began to push forward—one foot, then the other—inching toward the door. Her shaking fingers gripped the knob and turned. Ever so gently, she eased the door open, relieved to find an empty hallway. Gathering her courage, she stepped across the threshold.

A muscled arm snaked across her line of view, causing her to flinch as she drew back. The hand attached to the sinewy arm landed flat on the nearby wall as a warm body pressed into her uninjured side. Closing her eyes, she balled her fist, ready to strike.

"Not so fast there, slugger," a rugged baritone chimed in her ear, causing her to shiver. "You need rest before you charge back into the world—"

Swinging with all her might, Dani brought her fist high, aiming for the man's face. Although she didn't have time to align her blow, she aimed to strike his nose above the lips that had brushed her ear as he spoke.

The man's hand caught her fist, crushing it as he lowered her arm, causing her to cry out.

"You son of a bitch!"

"I don't want to hurt you, Dani," he said, his tone soothing even though her body was fraught with nerves and fear. "Take a deep breath and relax."

Lifting her gaze to his, she noted the silver flecks that glinted in his gunmetal gray eyes. His features were angular as he loomed over her although she was five feet, eight inches tall. She might not remember much, but for some reason, she remembered that.

"What do you want?" she asked, struggling to keep the fear from her voice. "Whatever it is, I'm sure we can negotiate."

His firm lips curved into a roguish smile, causing her knees to shake. Dark hair fell over his forehead, tinged with a bit of gray at the temples, and she had the insane thought he might be the most attractive man she'd ever seen. Dangerous. Mysterious. Hot.

"You try to negotiate every time," he murmured, lowering so his warm breath floated across her cheek. "It's so cute, babe."

Attempting to wrench her fist from his grasp, she glared at him until he released her. Drawing back, she let another blow fly, but he quickly caught her fist again, smirking as she writhed to break free.

"I know your tells by now, Dani. Believe me, you got me pretty good the first few times we did this, but now I can read your punches from a mile away. Don't get me wrong, it's sexy as hell when you try to slug me, but it's not conducive to moving the mission along."

"What mission?" she asked, infuriated by his tender endearments along with the fact he was all but *laughing* at her. "I have no idea who you are! If you want to kill me or...*worse*...then do it. But I'm certainly not involved in any sort of mission with you."

Something flashed in his eyes—tender and almost sad—before his grip relaxed on her fist. "I know this is scary. I'm sorry. It's my fault—"

"Why can't I remember anything? Did you drug me?"

Remorse crossed his features as he slowly shook his head. "It's your brain injury. You sustained it over three months ago, and your memory hasn't recovered."

"Three months? I've lost my memory for three months?"

"Yes," he softly confirmed. "You sustained it at your lab while you were working for Sendaxa."

Furrowing her brow, she tried to recall her last memory. "I don't work for Sendaxa. I work at Columbia University as a professor and head of their genetics lab." Pausing, she indexed her thoughts for any memory of working for the largest pharmaceutical company in the United States. "I vaguely remember receiving an email from an executive at Sendaxa expressing interest in working with me. That's all I remember about them."

Gray eyes assessed her as he nodded. "They recruited you to work on EverLife."

Blowing out a breath, she racked her brain, frustrated at the murky images that didn't quite form. "But I was so close to a cancer vaccine."

"Yes. Sendaxa offered you a deal: work for them to develop EverLife, and once it was approved for use, they would fund your cancer research."

Latching onto his gaze, she swallowed. "I'm assuming things didn't exactly go as planned."

Huffing a laugh, he shook his head. "You were successful in creating the EverLife formula but didn't realize it would be highly addictive. Once the side effects became known, you dedicated yourself to developing an addiction antidote. Cancer took a backseat to reversing the damage."

"Damage?" Dread filled her heart as her throat bobbed. "How much damage?"

Lifting his hand, he slowly extended it toward her cheek. Dani's brain screamed to recoil, but her body subconsciously leaned toward his.

Once he'd placed his rough palm over her cheek, his lips curved into a sad smile. "I'm happy to tell you everything, but you're hurt and I don't want to reopen your wound." Craning his neck, he eyed the side of her body with the laceration. "We have a protocol for when you wake up. I messed that up today and I'm sorry. I thought you'd sleep longer since you're recovering. I should know by now not to underestimate you."

Butterflies of anxiety flitted in her belly as she studied him. A strange desire to arch toward him and seek comfort in his muscular arms overwhelmed her. Squinting up at him, she asked, "Who are you to me?"

His broad lips twitched, causing her heart to slam between her ribs.

"One of these days, you're going to remember, and it will be the happiest day of my life, babe."

"Don't call me that," she said, feeling her nostrils flare. "I hate that endearment."

A deep chuckle rumbled in his chest. "I know. You seem to prefer 'slugger.' But I like 'babe.' Call me old-fashioned." Lifting his hand from her cheek, he tucked a strand of silky brown hair behind her ear.

"Please stop mocking me. I don't recognize you, but you seem so familiar..." Lifting her palms to her temples, she squeezed. "Fuck, my brain hurts."

"Hey," he murmured, gently encircling her wrists and dragging her hands away. Drawing her hands to his chest, he splayed one of her palms over each of his pecs. His heartbeat thrummed beneath her skin as he covered the backs of her hands with his. "It's okay, Dani. Look at me. *Feel* me."

Shallow breaths exited her lungs as his pulse ticked beneath her fingers. Staring deep into his stunning irises, she waited.

"Good," he soothed, lifting one hand to cup her jaw, stroking the skin with his thumb. "Who do you think I am?"

Her mouth opened and closed as she struggled to form words. "I have no idea. I have so many questions—"

"Do you remember my name?"

Tears stung her eyes as she shook her head. "I don't know you..."

Sighing, he removed his hand from her jaw before harshly rubbing his forehead. Lifting his gaze to hers, he said softly, "I'm Maverick."

Her features contorted. "Like *Top Gun*?"

Rolling his eyes, he scoffed. "Yes, like *Top Gun*. You ask me that every time I tell you my damn name. From the first time we met until right now. One day, you'll just accept that my parents were weird and gave their kid a strange name."

A laugh escaped her throat, surprising her as she stared up at the man who was both reassuring and mysterious. "When did we first meet?"

"Five years ago."

Dani gazed down, trying to remember.

"Since your brain injury, you only seem to remember as far back as your last days at Columbia and Sendaxa contacting you. But you don't ever remember moving to Bethesda to start the job."

Rapidly blinking, she worked to amalgamate the thoughts racing through her mind. Concern jolted down her spine as visions of her sisters' faces appeared. "Where are Raquel and Arianna?"

"Your sisters are safe," he assured, his tone calm. "They're here with us and you can see them, but first you need to rest. You're pretty banged up there, slugger."

Filled with trepidation—and a hefty surge of curiosity—she cemented her eyes to his. "Are we...lovers?"

White teeth flashed as he smiled, transforming his features into something so sexy her knees almost buckled.

"I guess you could say that..."

Narrowing her eyes, she regarded him.

"But I'm a lot more than your lover."

Swallowing thickly, she whispered, "You are?"

Nodding, he leaned closer, those swirling eyes searching hers.

"Danica Lawson, it's nice to meet you all over again. We do this dance every day, and it never gets old." Drawing back, he extended his hand. "Maverick Ward."

Tentatively shaking his hand, she tilted her head. "Maverick Ward...my lover...and..."

"Husband," he said, lips twitching at her rapid inhale. "I'm your husband, Dani. Pleasure to meet you, as always."

Suddenly, the floor seemed to melt away as the wound at her side throbbed. Unable to stand, she collapsed into her husband's arms, wondering if she would remember him the next time she regained consciousness.

Chapter 2

M averick caught his wife in his arms, careful of her wound, and lifted her as her head lolled.

"She fainted again?" a deep voice asked, attached to the man striding down the hallway.

"Yeah. I don't want to restrain her, but I might have to if she keeps waking up and trying to bolt."

Striding toward the bedroom, he placed Dani on the bed before tugging off her sneakers. Tossing them to the floor, he checked her wound before covering her with the comforter.

"Why didn't you leave the phone by her bed?" Dominic asked.

"I didn't think she'd wake this early. Her wound is healing, but the phone was almost dead last night so I decided to charge it. Rookie mistake," Maverick said. "If there's one thing we know about my wife, she's determined to escape every time she wakes up if the phone with the video she recorded isn't accessible." Grinning, he softly stroked her cheek. "For a geeky scientist, she's pretty badass."

"That's why we all love her," Dominic said quietly.

Maverick glanced at the man, six feet, six inches of thick, sinewed muscle under a buzz cut and austere features. A jagged scar ran from the corner of one eye, over his nose and ended at the opposite corner of his broad lips. Tattoos covered the arms crossed over his chest, and his dark eyes were filled with concern. It made sense considering one thing they both knew to be true: they both were in love with Maverick's wife.

An unspoken agreement lingered between Maverick and the stoic man with whom he'd forged a solid friendship over the years. They would never discuss Dominic's feelings as long as he never acted on them. It would be futile anyway considering Danica loved Maverick as fiercely as he loved her. Gazing at her, he stroked her chestnut-colored locks atop the pillow as she slept, thanking the universe she'd chosen him. Dominic was a good man, but for some reason, Dani had chosen Maverick.

Perhaps miracles were still possible.

Dominic and Maverick were aligned in the cause, and his friend was a damn good soldier, so Maverick was content to overlook the fact he was in love with his wife. He hoped that one day, once they set things straight and returned to some sense of normalcy, Dominic would find a woman who would capture his heart too. Only time would tell.

"Has Arianna returned from the scouting mission?" Maverick asked, tucking the covers around Dani's shoulders before rising.

"No, and she didn't take a comm device with her either," Dominic muttered, rubbing his forehead. "Stubborn woman. She looked me straight in the eye and told me she'd have one in her ear at all times, but I found it lying on the table by the front door. It's like she left it there to tell me to go fuck myself."

Breathing a laugh, Maverick cupped his chin. "I've never seen two people who detest each other work so brilliantly together. It defies logic. Half the time, I'm convinced she'd rather kill *you* than the Sen Force soldiers."

Dominic scoffed. "Or I'd rather kill her. I swear, most days I'm this close." He formed a circle with his hands, mimicking choking someone. "But then she usually ends up doing something cool, like protecting Raquel when she goes on her berry-picking excursions or kicking my ass when we spar, and I don't have the heart to go through with it."

Grinning, Maverick strode by his friend, gesturing with his head for the man to follow him so they could leave Dani to sleep and heal. As they trekked down the hallway, he patted Dominic's shoulder. "Are you admitting Arianna is a better fighter than you?"

Dominic's eyebrow arched. "I'll admit she's one of the best soldiers I've ever met. Better than me? No fucking way. But she's pretty damn awesome."

"That's a pretty big declaration from the best fighter *I've* ever met," Maverick said, entering the large back room of the abandoned home where they'd set up their temporary headquarters. "I have a feeling she'd say she was better than you, but who's keeping score?"

Dominic grunted in annoyance as they entered the makeshift lab Dani and Raquel had built in the den of the home they'd been residing in since Dani's brain injury.

"Where's Raquel?" Dominic asked, craning his neck to look outside. "I told her to stay inside until I was ready."

"She's obsessed with the mushrooms growing by the old shed," Maverick said, gesturing toward the window. "Maybe she's picking them."

"She's determined to recreate the antidote," Dominic said, craning his neck to look out the window.

"She was a preeminent biologist before the world went to shit, and I appreciate her trying to formulate an antidote," Maverick said, shaking his head. "But Dani is still our best hope...if her memory ever comes back."

"It will, Mav," Dominic said, cupping his shoulder. "And then we'll break into the Sendaxa lab to steal the secret antidote stash, and the world can begin to wake up from this nightmare."

"Raquel insists she can get Dani's memory back with some perseverance. The teas she concocts seem to help, and Dani logs everything," Maverick said, pointing to the notebook that sat beside the vials on the lab table. "Sometimes, when she looks at me, I see flashes of...*something* in her eyes. A small tendril of recognition, and that gives me hope."

"Never doubt the Lawson sisters," Dominic muttered. "If Raquel says Dani can get her memory back, I'm apt to believe it. Those three are stubborn as hell when they set their mind to something."

"No doubt, but I kind of dig that about Dani," Maverick said with a sly grin. "I love it when she tries to beat the crap out of me when she wakes up. It's hot."

"You're weird, man," Dominic said, shaking his head. "I'm going to head out and keep an eye on Raquel. Arianna and I haven't observed any Sen Force soldiers or deserters on any recent scouting missions, but I want to stay alert."

Before he could pivot and exit the room, a door slammed in the distance and heavy bootsteps echoed down the hallway. Arianna breezed in, silky dark hair hanging over one eye from the half of her head that wasn't shaved.

"Hey," she grunted, giving them both a quick salute. "Did Dani wake up?"

"The phone was charging so I blew it," Maverick said.

"Oh shit. Did she *Top Gun* you?" Amusement clouded her expression under her piercing hazel eyes.

"Yeah. She's a broken record with that one."

Nodding, Arianna crossed her arms and glowered at Dominic. "What the fuck is wrong with your face?"

With a sardonic eye roll, Dominic placed his hands on his hips. "You left your comm device behind again. You promised, Ari."

"Don't call me that," she snapped. "Only Dani calls me that. And why do you care?"

Thick nostrils flared as he studied her. "You know what? I don't. Go scout alone and get yourself killed for all I care."

She tilted her head, cheeks reddening with anger. "I would but I do need your back up *sometimes*," she snorted. "And Magic Mike over there can't do it because he needs to keep an eye on Dani."

"Am I Magic Mike in this scenario?" Maverick asked, pointing to his chest.

"Yep," Arianna said with a nod. "You and that pretty face. It's annoying. Try to be uglier, like this one." She pointed to Dominic. "Okay, I'm starving. The fields are clear, by the way. No Sen Force spies within a two-mile perimeter. The farmhouse has been our longest-lasting base, and I don't want to search for another one. For now, it's secure and they don't know we're here."

"Let's hope it lasts," Maverick said. "I'm going to make sure the phone is ready for the next time Dani wakes."

Arianna nodded before stomping out of the room toward the kitchen where they kept their meager food supplies.

Dominic grunted before pivoting and exiting as well.

"Lots of tension between those two," Maverick mumbled to himself, striding toward the table where vials, concoctions, and other supplies Raquel used to create her potential antidotes and teas resided. As he inspected the items, he reflected on the obvious distaste between his best friend and his wife's sister.

Narrowing his eyes, he drew a finger over one of the tea leaves as he pondered. Was it a love-hate thing? Maybe they just needed to have sex and see if that changed the dynamic. Chuckling, Maverick admitted that would certainly make things interesting, although it wasn't likely to happen.

Dominic fixated on Danica because she was safe. Easy. Unavailable. Exploring feelings for Arianna would open a Pandora's box he wasn't sure his friend would even consider. Dominic could be pretty oblivious and had one goal: to destroy the shell government that had taken over Washington, DC and restore the world to some semblance of normal. Dominic's sister had died of cancer, and he wanted to start a new chapter so Dani could finally develop her cancer vaccine.

But a man needed a release every once in a while, and Maverick wondered if his friend would eventually get tired of his own hand. The raw energy that vibrated between Dominic and Arianna was damn near combustible. They might kill each other if they had sex—but there were worse ways to go, Maverick mused, flattening his lips to contain his grin.

On that note, he needed to check on his wife and make sure he didn't fuck up again the next time she awoke. Turning, he approached her room, intent on making sure she didn't try to punch him when she regained consciousness.

Chapter 3

The next time Dani's eyes flew open, she shot up in bed, her hand darting to her laceration. It still marred her side, covered by the thick bandage, but she *remembered*. Maverick. Their conversation. The insane assertion he was her husband.

Baffling since she couldn't recall ever having met the man, and yet he seemed so familiar...

"Hey, sleeping beauty," the object of her musings said, striding into the room and pointing to the bed. "Mind if I sit?"

Dani blinked, wondering when she was going to wake up from the strangest dream she'd ever had. Clearing her throat, she nodded, unconsciously clenching the covers and drawing them higher.

Tilting his head, he studied her with those deep eyes. "You remember waking up before?"

"Yes," she rasped, her throat dry as the wound at her side throbbed. "How?"

Reaching into his pocket, he pulled out a cell phone and shook it. "I have the answer here."

"You're going to call someone?"

Huffing a laugh, he shook his head. "Most cell phone towers in America haven't worked in over a year, although some are still known to function, especially ones near the Sendaxa cities. The phone has some important videos, and

Arianna was smart enough to toss some chargers in her bag before we all went into hiding."

Dani glanced at the bedside lamp before reaching over and turning it on. "We still have electricity?"

"This place has a generator. Pretty fortuitous find. We've been staying here for months. Arianna and Dominic regularly patrol to ensure we're not on Sen Force's radar."

"Sen Force...?"

"Soldiers employed by Sendaxa to ensure the new world order they've created stays in place. Most are remnants of the old U.S. Army, which disbanded once the government collapsed."

Dani blinked once...twice...and once more for good measure before expelling a breath. "This is seriously the weirdest dream I've *ever* had."

His warm chuckle surrounded her, caressing her skin as tiny bumps rose along her arms. Somewhere in the far reaches of her mind, she remembered that laugh...rumbled in her ear as he covered her with his muscled body and kissed her until she breathed his name...

"Babe?"

Shaking her head to rid it of the madness, she scowled. "I really wish you wouldn't call me that."

A challenge flared in his eyes as he scooted closer. "Okay." Lifting the phone, he brought up a video before placing it in her hand. Leaning forward, he whispered, "But just so you know, there have been several times in the past when you *liked* when I called you that."

Bristling, she opened her mouth to give him a piece of her mind before he showed her his palms and stood. "Don't want to fight with you. Go on," he said, gesturing with his head. "Watch the video and we'll discuss after."

Shooting him one last glare, she pressed play on the video and gasped when she saw her own face.

"Hello, Dani. I know this is probably very shocking to you, but Maverick and I thought it was the best way to help you acclimate and navigate each day with your condition. Maverick is usually by your side when you watch this video, but if he's not, you'll meet him soon. I know it's hard to believe, but h

e is your husband and you can trust him. Take it from...well, yourself."

Dani's eyes darted to Maverick's before they lowered again. Heart racing, she concentrated on the sound of her own voice.

"I'm going to be succinct but try to hit all the important points. Maverick can fill in the time stamps and answer your questions afterward."

Pausing the video with shaking fingers, she asked, "How many days ago did I make this?"

"You made this video almost three months ago," Maverick said softly.

Lowering her gaze, she struggled to control her errant heartbeat and shallow breathing. "After my brain damage where I lost my memory."

"Yes." Rubbing his chin, he gestured with his head. "Keep going."

Pushing through the sticky fear that laced her veins, she pressed play.

"You most likely just asked Mav how long it's been since you made this video. I pray there aren't many days left you'll have to watch it."

Dani squirmed in the bed, straightening in an attempt to brace herself for what was to come.

"Several years ago, you were hired by a company called Sendaxa to spearhead a campaign to create a drug that could double human life expectancy. This drug was called EverLife. I'm going to assume Mav has explained this to you, but if not, pause here and he can."

Pausing the video, she scrunched her features as she contemplated. "I think I have the basics. Sendaxa recruited me to create EverLife, and I agreed on the contingency they would fund my cancer vaccine development afterward. It went terribly wrong and I created a highly addictive drug that was consumed by the masses."

Maverick crossed his arms over his thick chest and gave an affirmative nod.

Pursing her lips, she resumed the video.

"You were determined to eventually save humanity, and now—although it wasn't how you envisioned it—you have your chance."

Glancing at Maverick, she asked, "I assume this is the mission you were referring to?"

"Yep. Your sisters and my friend Dominic are all on our team, and we've been living in this abandoned farmhouse while we figure out next steps. I'll explain more after you finish."

Clicking the screen, she continued watching. "*EverLife's addictive side effects were worse than any drug ever created. The need for the drug began to overtake people from all walks of society. They left their jobs and families, consumed with finding the drug on the black market as it became sold out in pharmacies. Sendaxa tasked you to create an antidote to counteract the side effects, which you did.*"

"Wait," Dani said, sitting up straighter in the bed. "If we have an antidote, what the hell are we doing here? Let's cure everyone and get back to normal."

"It's not that easy, sweetheart," he said, resignation in his voice.

Frustration swamped her as she resumed the video.

"*As the addiction spread, society began to break down. Homeless addicts roamed the streets, and the worldwide economy could no longer function. Sendaxa's CEO, Luthor Cromwell, gained immense power while the government was simultaneously indicting him on charges of duping the public about EverLife's addictive tendencies. He saw an opportunity to escape persecution by destroying the government.*"

"Holy shit," Dani whispered, overwhelmed by the unbelievable story.

"*Using the vast wealth he'd made from EverLife, Luthor closed off the major cities, fortifying them and ensuring only people inside the walls had the antidote. The ones who remained outside were left to die. The people inside the cities were given a watered-down antidote that offers small relief but doesn't cure the addiction. Your only hope is to retrieve the full-strength antidote you created, replicate it, and begin distributing it. You try every day to recreate it in the makeshift lab you and Raquel created, but you've been unsuccessful so far. You need the original antidote to duplicate it effectively."*

Tears stung her eyes as her chin began to warble. "So many people are suffering...because of me. Why haven't I retrieved the antidote yet?"

Maverick stepped closer and tapped the phone to pause the video. "The world is in shambles, Dani. The wealthy retreated inside their fortified walls, able to continue their use of the drug and survive with the modified antidote, although I'd barely call that survival. Those left outside the walls with no antidote suffered most of all. Societies across the globe fell, and the world is now composed of those who live in the fortified cities and those who fend for themselves on the outside. Villages and towns have formed outside the cities, mostly run by connected dealers who can supply addicts with black-market substitutes for EverLife."

"Then we have to go now," she said, tossing the phone on the bed and throwing off the covers, attempting to stand. "I have to retrieve the antidote—"

"Whoa," he said, gently gripping her shoulders and urging her back against the headboard. "That's what we're trying to do, Dani. Three months ago, you attempted to steal a secret stockpile of the antidote from the Sendaxa lab so you could replicate it. Unfortunately, someone banged you on the head before you could retrieve the stash, and we went on the run until we figure out a solution."

"Well, let's go back and break in again," she said, exasperated. "I'm ready."

Breathing a laugh, he shook his head. "There are reasons why we haven't done that yet, sweetheart."

"Being?"

"The lab where you created the antidote is under Sen Force security. You set up some extra security measures to ensure no one but you could access the hidden antidote."

"Shit." Harshly rubbing her forehead with her fingers, she said, "I would've set up a secure keypad with a numerical security code only I knew."

"Along with a separate keypad that only opens if touched by your index finger. It reads temperature and pulse to prevent someone from chopping off your finger and using it while...not attached to you," he finished, arching a brow.

"Wow," she said, lips flapping as she expelled a breath. "I was resourceful."

Admiration entered his gaze as he grinned. "Yep. As head of security at the lab, I was able to approve the extra security measures without Luthor Cromwell's knowledge. That kept it under the radar."

Her shoulders crumpled as she sank into the bed. "Don't tell me I didn't write down the security code once you installed the keypad. I must've emailed it to myself...or made a jump drive with the information?"

Gently tapping her forehead, he gave a soft grin. "Everything only exists here. You were too paranoid to write things down and prided yourself on your photographic memory. When society began to crumble, you were afraid to email anything to yourself or write notes in your phone. Sendaxa essentially took over the government, and you didn't want the secret antidote stash to be discovered."

Harshly rubbing a hand over her face, she groaned. "I can't believe they talked me into working for them. They must've really played on my desire to cure cancer."

"They knew about your mom," he said, lowering to sit beside her before sliding his hand over her leg and squeezing through the covers. "They're a company with limitless means and investigated you thoroughly before they recruited you. They knew you were the best geneticist in your field and understood how devastating your mom's death was. They preyed on your nobility, and it worked."

"Son of a bitch. And now I have amnesia."

"And now you have amnesia," he affirmed with a slow nod. "You were hit in the head the night you tried to steal the antidote. We still don't know who injured you. Dominic found you unconscious on the floor before we carried you out and went on the run."

She stared blankly at the phone as she tried to digest the overwhelming information. "I need to remember the code so we can break in again and steal the antidote."

"Bingo," he said with a nod. "We don't have the tools or compounds out here to replicate the antidote—although Raquel might die trying—but if you got your hands on a vial, you'll duplicate it in a heartbeat."

"I will," she said confidently, "with Raquel's help. But I definitely need the sample. Damn it."

Taking her hand, he slid his palm over hers, the skin coarse and warm. "Which is why we're trying like hell to restore your memory."

Shaking the phone, she narrowed her eyes. "How did you convince me to make this video?"

"Every once in a while, we have a good day where you're able to let your guard down by the end of the night and trust me. They're rare but they happen."

"And we had one of those days and you had the idea to make the video?"

"*You* had the idea," he said, cocking a brow, "and it was brilliant. Watching the video seems to help you trust me."

Dani allowed her eyes to rove over his face, wishing she recognized this man who claimed to be her husband. He was sinfully handsome and stared back at her with deep emotion. Although the situation was disconcerting, he truly seemed to care for her. Deciding to lighten the moment, she lifted her brows. "If this is some elaborate ruse to get laid, you get an A-plus for effort."

Tossing back his head, laughter bellowed from his throat. His neck was thick with a prominent Adam's apple, and a vision of trailing wet kisses along the skin there flashed through her brain. It was...*familiar*...as if her lips had already traveled the path a thousand times before...

"Babe, you've been through the ringer, but you never lose your sense of humor." Taking the phone, he set it on the nightstand before clutching both her hands and squeezing. "God, I miss you so much. I think it's only a matter of time before your memory returns."

Licking her parched lips, she asked, "Are Raquel and Ari okay?"

"They're both fine and valuable members of our team. Arianna and Dominic perform scouting missions to make sure we're safe, and Raquel is continuing your work when you're not able to help."

"She's an exceptional biologist and botanist."

Nodding, he scooted closer and craned his neck to look at her side. "How's your side feeling?"

"It hurts but I'll survive." Glancing down, she asked, "How was I injured anyway?"

"You and Raquel went out to pick some berries on the outskirts of the farm. Dominic was keeping watch and heard a sound in the distance that alarmed him. It ended up being nothing, but he sent you and Raquel back to the house so he could check it out. You tripped on a log and fell straight into an old pitchfork lying on the ground." Shaking his head, he sighed. "You have some terrible luck, Dani. I wouldn't suggest *ever* playing the lottery."

Laughing, she leaned farther back on the bed, snuggling into the soft mattress. "Seriously. So, do I lose my memory nightly? Is that why I remember our encounter earlier?"

"Yes." Resignation laced his features as his thumb tenderly skated over her skin. "You can take short naps and retain memories during a one-day span, but after a longer sleep, you always wake up unable to remember." Lifting his hand, he tucked a strand of hair behind her ear. "I'm so sorry. I hate it for you."

Curiosity squeezed her throat as a multitude of questions swirled in her mind. Gathering her courage, she asked, "Do we...sleep together?"

That sexy smile overtook his lips as he slowly dragged the pad of his thumb over the back of her hand.

"Sometimes. We did the night you made that video. Sometimes we sleep together..." leaning forward, he whispered, "*and sometimes we even have sex...*"

Air rushed from her lungs as she assessed him. "How in the hell did we end up together?"

Laughing, he dragged a hand over his face. "Wow. Are you trying to decimate my ego?"

"The opposite," she rushed to assure him. "I'm a workaholic scientist and you're"—waving her hand over his body, she struggled to speak—"the hottest guy I've ever seen. I can't imagine a scenario where we would've ever crossed paths."

His low-toned chuckle caused sparks of arousal to ignite deep within, and she squeezed her thighs together. "I was head of security for the Sendaxa lab. We met when you took the job." Lifting her hand, he grazed a kiss over her knuckles. "I guarded you when you worked, and since you're a workaholic, that meant I spent a lot of time with you. As we got to know each other, we fell in love."

Tilting her head, her eyebrows drew together as she allowed her eyes to assess his muscular frame. "It's a nice story. I'd love to hear the details sometime."

"Anytime. I never get tired of telling you that story."

Swallowing thickly, she gazed into his eyes, unable to look away. "You must know I love tulips," she said with a cheeky grin. "Just trying to think of ways I can help you get on my good side."

"I do," he said, winking and sending a rush of elation through her veins. "And chocolate. And being touched right here..." Eyes cemented to hers, he gently placed the pads of his fingers on her collarbone before lightly tracing the skin there.

Licking her suddenly dry lips, Dani sat frozen as the most gorgeous man she'd ever seen caressed her rapidly heating skin.

"You like me to go lower too," he murmured, running his finger along the neckline of her black tank top. "Eventually, you always ask me to kiss you...here." Never breaking their gaze, he ran his finger over the mound of her breast above the fabric. "You're *very* sensitive here, Dani."

Clearing her throat, she lowered her gaze to his hand. He let it rest for another moment before withdrawing it. "But I think that's enough for today."

Overcome with the need to fan herself, Dani sank into the bed, determined not to showcase her arousal. It was just too...confusing...and hot...and weird...

"Today's pretty much shot, so I'd suggest you continue to rest before dinner." Rising, he urged her to lie back and covered her with the blankets. "After that, we'll do it all again tomorrow, but I'm not going to mess up the routine." Lifting the phone, he shook it.

"Okay," she whispered, wondering why she could still feel the heat of his touch on her skin. Rapid heartbeats pounded as he smiled down at her. Reaching over, he clicked off the bedside lamp. "I'll wake you before dinner. Sweet dreams." Turning to leave, he paused when she called his name.

"Hmm?" he asked, facing her.

"I'm sensitive behind the knees too, especially my left one where the birthmark is."

His lips quirked as he studied her in the dim light shining through the curtains. "Your birthmark is behind your *right* knee, sweetheart, but good try. And believe me, I know you're sensitive behind both of them. Good night."

His broad shoulders exited the room, leaving the door cracked behind him, and Dani pulled the covers to her chest, unable to control her grin. The birthmark had been a test, which Maverick had passed.

"Holy shit, Dani," she whispered, closing her eyes to steady herself. "You have a husband and he's...probably the sexiest man on Earth. How did you manage that?"

Overwhelmed with questions, she allowed them to flit through her head as she attempted to catalog them all. Of course, the effort was futile since she wouldn't remember a damn one of them when she awoke the next morning.

Chapter 4

A rianna Lawson waited for the house to get dark and quiet. She rarely slept, so she figured instead of wasting hours lying in bed staring at the ceiling, she'd let everyone else fall asleep before heading out. She'd noticed something during her scouting session earlier and wanted to check it out. Since she didn't deem it a threat, she hadn't told anyone else, but it still lingered in her mind hours later, which meant it required attention.

Once midnight hit, she rose, tossing on some of the black clothing she'd managed to stuff into her bag before they all went into hiding the night Dani lost her memory. Arianna preferred black, perhaps because it was the color of her thick, straight hair—well, the half she kept, at least.

She'd shaved the other half of her head bald on a whim once she left the army. Something about choosing her own damn hairstyle was freeing. The remaining half had grown long and often fell over her eye unless she twisted it in a braid. Striding to the hazy mirror in the room she'd claimed in the farmhouse, she began twining the strands, wanting it off her face for tonight's excursion. Once the tip was secured in a rubber band, she gazed at her greenish-brown eyes in the mirror.

"Well, you're not winning any beauty contests, Ari," she muttered, "but you could probably kick the shit out of the judges." Snickering, she secured her gun and knife to her belt and headed downstairs to the foyer by the front door, careful that her boots remained silent on the wooden steps.

Stopping by the front table, she picked up the tiny comm device, examining it between her fingers as she debated wearing it. No one would be listening on the other end anyway. Dominic was usually her comm partner, but he was sleeping. The tiny devices communicated like walkie-talkies and didn't require any telecommunication equipment. Good thing since most telecom equipment no longer worked.

"Fuck it," she murmured, setting it back on the table. "You'll be back in an hour, and they'll never even know you were gone." Grabbing her backpack, she headed to the kitchen and stuffed the bag full of apples, strawberries and some of the chicken Raquel had cooked for dinner. Finding an abandoned house with a generator had been a godsend, and Arianna only took the appropriate amount of food she knew the others wouldn't notice.

Trailing back to the front door, she reached for the knob and froze when someone cleared their throat behind her. Annoyed, she glanced toward the ceiling in frustration before turning to face Dominic.

His face was a jagged piece of beauty, anger marring the smooth skin that surrounded the ragged scar that ran from his eye, across his angular nose, to the other side of his perfectly full lips. He should've been ugly. God, she wished he were. But her heart leapt in her chest like the traitorous organ did every time he approached her.

Of course it did.

Because Arianna was deeply, inexplicably, unavoidably in love with Dominic Cavalleri.

And he was in love with her sister.

Furious at the feelings she couldn't contain, Arianna bristled and lifted her chin. "Can I help you?"

Scoffing, he strode closer and jabbed his finger toward her face. "Are you fucking serious?" he hissed. "You're going out alone after midnight? Do you have a death wish?"

"Don't point your finger in my face!" she whispered, swatting it away before gesturing upstairs. "I don't want to wake anyone up. I'll be back hours before sunrise."

Crossing his arms over his chest, he glowered at her as he tapped his bare foot. Arianna stared back, determined to maintain his unwavering gaze. He thought he was tough? She'd stare him down all fucking night long. She was stubborn as hell and certainly not intimidated by a man whose ass she could kick any day and twice on Sunday.

Probably. Of course, he was bigger than her, which was a feat since she was almost six feet tall and a hundred and sixty pounds of pure muscle. No one would ever accuse Arianna of being a shrinking violet, that was for damn sure.

Even though Dominic was several inches taller and built like a freight train, she'd sparred with him enough to know his tells. He was a good fighter and incredibly strong—but she was faster. Better at adapting and shifting tactics in the heat of a battle. He wasn't a bad soldier—hell, he was probably the best she'd seen, besides herself—but he wasn't invincible. And if she had to physically take him on in order to accomplish what she meant to do, she would without hesitation.

Sighing, he swiped a hand over his chin and shook his head. "Stay here." Pivoting, he began to walk away.

"Um, I'm not sure who you think you're talking to, but I don't take orders from you—"

"Shut up," he rasped, turning and slicing a hand through the air. "Do you want to wake the whole house up? I'm going with you. I just need to get dressed. Don't fucking move."

Crossing her arms, she huffed as her features contorted into a mask of annoyance. Although she didn't take orders from anyone, she'd also learned Dominic was as stubborn as she was and didn't want to waste time arguing. "Fine. Hurry the fuck up."

Shooting her one last glare, he pivoted and strode toward the small bedroom on the opposite side of the kitchen. He'd claimed it when they moved in, probably because it was on the ground floor near Dani's. She had some valuable info inside her head, and Dominic was in love with her, so it made sense. Arianna was fine sleeping upstairs, as did Raquel and Maverick on the nights Dani didn't trust him enough to bang him. Poor Mav. He did his best to win her over every day. Arianna had respect for him. He hadn't wavered in his dedication to Dani once. Maybe true love existed after all—for women like Dani, of course.

Craning her neck to look in the mirror that hung in the foyer, Arianna reminded herself it was okay men didn't think about her that way. Women like her didn't get roses and poems. They got scowls from men who were intimidated pussies because she was a better soldier. Fine with her. She'd use her skills to protect their team until Dani regained her memory and they'd retrieved the antidote from the lab.

Then Arianna would let Dani and Raquel heal the world while she retreated somewhere quiet and serene. She'd conceive through artificial insemination and have the child she craved without ever needing a man. It was a solid plan and one she planned to see to fruition once the mission was accomplished. For someone like her who had no blood relatives, it had become extremely important somewhere along the way to have a child. Someone who shared an unbreakable connection to her.

A twinge of guilt flared in her chest as Cynthia Lawson's beautiful face appeared in her mind. Her adoptive mother had always treated Arianna as her own and never made her feel different. She'd taken Arianna in when her birth parents had died in a car accident when she was only four years old. Their will had designated custody to Arianna's maternal grandmother, her only living relative at the time it was written. Unfortunately, Arianna's grandmother had passed of natural causes six months before her parents' accident, and they hadn't rewritten the will at the time of her death.

With no other relatives to take her in, Arianna was set to be shuffled into the foster system. Cynthia had been friends with her parents and lived next door. The kind woman had petitioned the court for custody of Arianna and given her a home. It had been one of the best turns of fortune in Arianna's life, and she was extremely thankful.

But still, in the hidden corners of her heart, she wanted someone who was...*hers*. True family, related by blood. Since she was a few months shy of forty, she really needed to get on that because the window to pop out a kid closed a fraction every day. But first, she needed to complete the mission and ensure they retrieved the antidote.

Mission, then baby. Lifting her brows in the reflection, she nodded. "Good plan, Ari."

"Sounds like a titillating conversation you're having with yourself out here," Dominic muttered, stalking down the dim hallway.

Shooting him the bird, she resisted the urge to tell him to go to hell. Those broad lips just smirked, driving her insane, so she turned and opened the door. Dominic followed behind, quietly securing the multitude of locks he and Maverick had installed. Hesitating, he lifted his gaze to her, his deep brown orbs swimming with concern. "Maybe we should tell Mav before we go."

"He's a trained soldier just like we are," she said, walking down the wooden porch stairs. "And you don't have to come. You're not invited anyway." Approaching the mist-covered grass, she began walking toward the gravel road that led to the woods, which were her destination.

When she approached the protective fence she, Dominic and Maverick had built, she carefully opened the barbed-wired gate. The circular perimeter wasn't perfect, but it added an extra layer of protection around their temporary home. Closing the gate behind them, she resecured the rope that held it closed and headed into the darkness.

Dominic fell into step beside her, his presence comforting, which annoyed her. If she were honest, she'd admit that having him near her sent a smooth wave of warmth throughout her entire body. His scent always seemed to invade her nostrils—crisp like the evergreen trees that grew in her back yard as a kid. It was...calming...refreshing...*sexy*...

Tamping down her unwanted attraction, she remained silent as she traipsed over the gravel and into the forest. Dominic followed her without a word, and something coiled deep in her belly at his silent faith in her even though he didn't have a clue where they were headed.

"I spotted a clearing with some sleeping bags, blankets and a banked fire," she said softly, feeling the need to explain. "There was a soccer ball nearby. I think there are some addicts living out here, and they have a kid...or kids. If so, I want to leave them some food."

Dominic glanced at her from the corner of his eye before nodding. "Okay."

Rolling her eyes, she continued walking under the dense canopy of leaves from the surrounding trees. "I don't need protection. You should've stayed home and kept an eye on Dani. She's the one who's integral to our mission."

Dominic remained silent, which drove her a thousand shades of crazy. Thinning her lips, she told herself she didn't owe him any explanations.

"You're important too, Ari," he finally said, the words sending shivers of pleasure through every cell of her skin. "I need you. Maverick and I couldn't do this on our own. Even with the three of us, we're outnumbered, but I like our chances better with you on our side." Reaching over, he squeezed her upper arm. "So stop doing stupid shit like scouting alone and going on secret missions without me. We're a team."

It was a warm summer night, so Arianna had only donned a black tank top, leaving her arms bare against the night air. As Dominic's palm covered her exposed skin, she felt herself flush and desperately wanted to pull away. God, she wished he wouldn't touch her. It swirled too many murky feelings deep in her core she'd never be able to extinguish.

"Thanks for your help," she mumbled, drawing her arm away and slightly shaking it, as if to shake off the remnants of his touch. "I know how much you want to protect Dani, and I'll keep doing my part."

A slow breath exited his lips as leaves and twigs crunched underneath their boots. Arianna sensed frustration in the soft breath, as well as longing and something else she couldn't quite identify. Finally, he said, "You don't have to throw it in my face all the time, you know? I understand she's Mav's. I know you don't give a shit about emotion, but some of us feel it even if we don't want to."

If he only knew. Squeezing her eyes closed for a brief moment, she wondered what he would do if she turned to face him and professed her love for the entire forest to hear. Considering he thought she hated him and was in love with her sister, he'd probably toss his head back and laugh in her face until his fucking lungs collapsed. Because if there was one thing Arianna had learned a long time ago, it was that men would never want a declaration of love from her.

She'd learned it from her high school boyfriend, who'd thoughtlessly taken her virginity and then laughed in her face when she exclaimed her love for him afterward.

From her college boyfriend, whom she discovered had a fantastic ass from behind...when she came home to find him fucking her roommate.

And from the man who'd proposed to her with such zeal over a decade ago. The soldier in her squadron who'd convinced her he loved her...until she'd realized he saw sleeping with her as the fastest way to move up the ranks.

Three attempts at love, which Arianna considered a full execution of the "three strikes and you're out" rule. She'd tried. She'd failed. She'd learned to never put her feelings on display for a man *ever* again. End of story. Thank you, drive through, please.

"Emotion isn't something I have time for," she said, swiping a branch out of their path as they walked down a haphazard trail. "But I'll try to leave you alone about Dani. Sucks to want something you can't have, but that's life, I guess."

He surprised her by snickering, and she craned her head to look at him, unable to control her corresponding smile. "What?"

"I just think it's funny to hear you say you'll let up on me. It's never going to happen." Grasping a low branch, he lifted it high and urged her to walk underneath it before he followed her. "I think you live to razz me, Ari."

"Don't call me Ari," she said, shooting him a glare over her shoulder, although her tone was light. "It's a nickname meant for people who care about me. Only my sisters call me that."

His broad fingers encircled her arm, drawing her to a stop and tugging her slightly closer. Those gorgeous eyes stared into her own, the hurt simmering there illuminated by the soft moonlight above. "I care about you, Arianna. Even though I want to strangle you most of the time, I care about you."

Huffing a laugh, she drew his arm away, her own palm on fire from the contact with the prickly hairs. "Wow, you're really in the feels tonight. It's weird." Glancing toward the nearby clearing, she gestured with her head. "Come on. The camp I spotted is in that clearing. Let's go."

She lurched ahead, needing to create space between them so she didn't drown in the warm heat of his body or the heady evergreen scent that shot straight to the place between her thighs. Determined to remain indifferent, she approached the campsite, noticing the pale glow of the fire. A woman and girl were nestled in two sleeping bags on the far side, and a boy, who Arianna guessed to be eight or nine, sat beside the fire, cradling bent legs as he stared into the flames. His chin rested on his knees as he slowly rocked back and forth, and sympathy swelled as she noticed how skinny he was.

"Hey," she whispered, holding up a hand when he gasped. Wide eyes latched onto hers, laced with fear and surprise.

"Don't be scared," she said, her soft tone reassuring. Slowly approaching, she crouched before him. "I'm Arianna and that's Dominic." She pointed over her shoulder. "He's really ugly, but he's harmless."

Dominic scoffed behind her, and the boy's shoulders seemed to relax slightly. Gripping the straps, she slowly eased the backpack off her shoulder. "Is that your mom and sister?"

He nodded, looking toward their sleeping forms before resuming eye contact with Arianna. "She's sick from the medicine she took. We live out here since we lost our house."

Nodding, Arianna slid the backpack over the ground as the boy warily watched her. "We brought you some food. Figured you might be hungry." The boy's eyes gleamed with hope, and she grinned. "It's okay. I'll leave the bag here but only if you'll share with your mom and sister when they wake up."

The boy nodded his head with vigor as he reached over, grabbing the bag and tugging it toward him. Unzipping it, he sucked in a breath as he observed the contents inside. Pulling out the container with the strawberries, he took a huge bite, his lips curving as he began to chew.

"How long have you been staying here?"

Squinting one eye, he stared up at the sky. "A few days. Mom says that once she feels better, we're going to walk to the compound where her brother lives. They take in people who need the medicine like she does."

Anger flared in Arianna's chest as she took a moment to rail at the state of the world. The entire fabric of society collapsed because people wanted to take a drug to stay young forever. Now, most of them were battered and broken by addiction and would die meaningless deaths. So much destruction because people wanted to play God with their own bodies. It was a terrible tragedy she hoped to end before humanity reached the point of no return.

Only time would tell if she would succeed.

"It's time to go," Dominic said, cupping Arianna's shoulder and urging her to rise. "Safe travels to the compound, son. I hope your mom feels better."

"Thank you for the food," he said, lifting the strawberry and waving. "I promise I'll share."

A twig snapped to Arianna's right, causing her to surge to her feet. Dominic rose beside her, heat emanating from his large frame as they gazed into the dark woods.

"Sen Force?" Dominic asked softly.

"I didn't see any evidence when I scouted, but I could've missed it—"

A loud bang sounded a millisecond before a bullet whizzed by her ear. Grasping the gun at her waist, she drew, aiming at the dense forest. Dominic drew his gun and tried to step in front of her as the woman and girl beside the fire jolted awake and screamed.

"Protect the camp," she said, pushing in front of Dominic and stepping toward the brush where the shot commenced. "I'll check it out."

"Ari…" Dominic warned.

"Come out and face us!" she yelled, squinting at the man she could barely see hiding behind a tree set a few feet into the clearing. "Coward!"

The man slowly edged away from the tree, gun held high as he aimed at Arianna. They faced off, hands gripping their weapons, as he entered the campsite.

"I'm not Sen Force," the man said in a gravelly voice. Judging by the deep wrinkles around his eyes and parched lips, Arianna surmised he hadn't had proper shelter or water in some time.

"Well, you have a gun and I'm not feeling real friendly right now," she said through clenched teeth.

"I'm a deserter," he said, moving forward as Arianna lifted the gun to aim between his eyes. "And I need some EverLife. I know the woman has some stashed in her bag. I've been following them for two days."

"I only have enough left to get to my brother's compound," the woman pleaded, holding her daughter as they rocked on the ground. "I need a fix every few hours or I'll die."

"Lady," the man said, lifting his gun and aiming it directly at her. "I hate to tell you this, but you're already dead."

A loud growl shot through the forest before Dominic barreled into the man's side, knocking him to the ground. Arianna had observed him creeping up on the deserter as the situation unfolded. Another shot was fired, and Arianna urged the family to scurry behind her as she trained the gun on the men.

They rolled and scuffled, each grunting as they punched and kicked. Arianna's heart pounded as she tried to find a clean shot that wouldn't hit Dominic.

Suddenly, Dominic seized control of the man's gun, pressing the barrel to his temple and firing a fatal blow. The deserter crumpled beneath him, muscles turning lax as Dominic expelled a deep breath.

"Damn it," he breathed, rising and planting a fist on his hip. "I didn't want to kill him."

Arianna rushed over, lowering to place two fingers on his neck. "Well, you did, and I'm glad. He sealed his fate when he deserted Sen Force." She tapped her fingers on the brand that had been burned into his neck. The one all deserters were forced to bear before being exiled from the District.

"Mama," a high-pitched voice cried.

"I'm here, baby," the woman soothed, pulling both children into her sides as they sat on the ground.

"You should have enough food in the bag I gave your son to get to your brother's compound," Arianna said, facing them. "I'd go now. You'll be less detectable in the dark."

The woman rose, extending shaking hands to her children. "Come on. Let's go."

The boy grabbed the food sack and the small pack that must've held their meager belongings. After grasping his mother's hand, the boy turned to look over his shoulder as she led them away. His eyes shone with fear and gratitude as they locked onto Arianna's. His soundless *thank you* almost broke the heart that had hardened into a lifeless rock years ago.

Once they disappeared, she sighed and rubbed her forehead. "Fuck. We probably made too much noise. Do you think we're blown?"

"I don't know, but we need to bury the body," Dominic said, approaching her. "This is why—"

"I swear to god," she interjected, holding up a hand. "If you lecture me right now on why this was a bad idea, I'll shoot you. Those kids needed food."

Deep brown eyes darted between hers before he nodded. "Okay. Let's head back, get a shovel, and finish this while the moon's still high."

Nodding, she fell into step beside him, shoulders drooping at the disastrous turn of events. Closing her eyes, she sent out a soft prayer for the family's safety. Arianna wasn't religious, but she figured it sure as hell wouldn't hurt.

They each grabbed a shovel from the shed behind the farmhouse and returned to the site. The fire burned low, the remaining shards of wood glowing a deep orange. Glancing toward the spot where they'd left the body, Arianna's eyes grew wide as her spine straightened with alarm.

The body they'd left dead and cold upon the grass was gone.

An hour later, after thoroughly searching the site and surrounding woods, Arianna and Dominic stood beside the now-banked fire. Hands upon their hips, they both absently stared at the charred wood, Arianna gnawing her lip as she debated.

"There are no footprints and no evidence of the body being dragged," she said. "He literally disappeared."

"The only explanation is that someone—or a group of people—lifted him and carried him away."

"Who would rescue a deserter's body?" she asked, lifting her gaze to his. "Certainly not Sen Force."

"It makes no sense," Dominic said, shaking his head. "But it's got to be close to three a.m., and we're both beat. Let's come back tomorrow and examine the site in the daylight. We're not going to accomplish anything tonight."

Defeated, Arianna nodded and began the trek home. Regret coiled in her stomach, mostly because her intended good deed had turned horribly wrong. Two kids were now traveling in the dark, scared and vulnerable.

"They weren't safe in the open either, Ari," Dominic said, reaching over and squeezing her hand. "They won't be safe until they get to the compound. It's probably better that you spurred them along."

Taking comfort for one small moment, she squeezed his hand. "I'll choose to believe that. Thank you."

They reached the porch steps, the wood creaking under their boots as they climbed. After resting the shovels against the porch wall, they entered the darkened house. Arianna kicked off her boots as Dominic clicked the locks behind her. Straightening, she almost banged into the thick wall of his chest. His broad hands gripped her upper arms, steadying her as she cursed herself for taking off the boots here instead of in her room. Without them, she was an inch shorter, causing her to feel vulnerable next to his thick frame.

"Let's return to the site at seven a.m. sharp. Good night." She turned to bolt up the stairs as his hand snaked around her arm. Whirling back, she opened her mouth to tell him that if he ever grabbed her again, she was going to punch his nose clean off his face.

But his expression froze her, turning every muscle in her body to stone. He was gazing at her with an intensity and...*respect*. It unnerved her to her very core.

"It was noble to take food to the kids, Ari," he said softly. "We'll figure out who moved the deserter's body. We knew we wouldn't be able to hide here forever."

"We need to tell Mav."

He gave a curt nod. "We'll tell everyone tomorrow. You and I will go back to examine the site and leave Dani and Raquel to work on science-y stuff. We'll stay on high alert."

Arianna's lips twitched. "Science-y stuff? Is that a technical term?"

A dark eyebrow arched, causing her heart to lurch. Why did she find him so fucking sexy?

"It's all I've got." Lifting his hands, he took a step back. "Don't beat yourself up about tonight. You're too hard on yourself. You're a good one, Ari."

She wanted to be angry at his continued use of her nickname, but her throat was suddenly tight with a thousand emotions she couldn't name and desperately wanted to eliminate. Unable to stop herself, she asked, "A good what?"

His eyes roved over her face, lowering to her neck and the rapidly reddening skin above her collarbone before lifting back to hers. Leaning closer, he whispered, "A good soul, no matter how mean you are. You might fool everyone else, but you can't fool me."

Straightening her spine, she swallowed the lump in her throat and forced herself to speak. "You don't know me. Don't pretend you do." Turning, she began to head up the stairs before turning back and lifting a finger. "And if you ever grab my arm again, I'll chop off your fucking hand. Got it?"

Those broad lips twitched before slowly curving into the sexiest smile Arianna had ever seen. Convinced her knees were going to collapse, she pivoted and resumed walking up the stairs.

"With a knife or a saw?" he taunted, his gruff voice washing over her as she tackled the stairs. "Just so I'm prepared..."

Extending her middle finger, she shot him one last silent "Fuck you" before cresting the second floor. She quickly washed her hands and face in the upstairs bathroom, thankful for the running water. Striding into her bedroom, she tugged off her pants and shirt and climbed between the sheets clad in her underwear and bra. As she relaxed, she stared at the ceiling, hoping like hell she hadn't blown their cover.

Minutes later, she turned on her side and forced her eyes closed, determined to sleep. As she drifted, she imagined Dominic's warm body cradling her as that deep voice whispered in her ear...

You're a good one, Ari...such a good girl for me...

Groaning, she punched the pillow before eventually falling into a restless slumber.

CHAPTER 5

Maverick rose with the sun the next morning and entered Dani's room, careful to remain quiet. There was a note he liked to leave by the phone so she'd see it when she awoke, and he placed it on the nightstand before exiting.

Open the camera app and watch the first video, then come and find me.

Love, Maverick.

Heading to the kitchen, he brewed some of the tea the previous owners had stashed in the pantry. They'd been stocked full, and Maverick was grateful for that. Sadly, they'd run out of coffee after their first month in the farmhouse, which had led to an overall rise in morning crankiness for everyone. Now, after several months, he'd gotten used to the tea and was thankful they'd found a place with a generator and working well in the back yard.

The kettle began to boil, and he turned off the stove before pouring the tea and dunking the bag into the scalding liquid. Returning to the sink, he stared out the window at the shed and the meadow beyond. They'd been lucky, remaining off the grid in the abandoned home, but Maverick knew that luck always ran out.

The time to break into Sendaxa's lab and retrieve Dani's secret antidote was near. If she didn't regain her memory, they'd have to forge ahead and try like hell to succeed.

"Good morning," Raquel's sweet voice chimed, and Maverick turned to smile at his wife's youngest sister. Arianna looked nothing like Dani or Raquel since she was adopted, but the two younger sisters bore a resemblance to each other. They shared the same light green eyes, although Dani's had gorgeous honey-colored flecks that were absent in Raquel's, and both had a smattering of freckles across their nose and cheeks. Dani was stunning in an almost ethereal way, with her pert nose, bright smile and thick brown hair...but of course, he was biased because he was her husband.

Raquel was pretty in a more muted way, and Maverick had heard her say on many occasions that Arianna got the brawn, Dani got the looks and the brains, and she'd gotten the baby fat along with a hefty side of awkwardness. It was a self-deprecating statement she made with a teasing grin, but it always stirred compassion inside Maverick's heart. Raquel was a sweet, loving person who was a fantastic scientist in her own right, and he hated it when she disparaged herself.

"Good morning to you," he said, noticing she was wearing sneakers. "You must be planning an early-morning walk."

"Yeah," she said, trailing over to pour some water before stuffing a tea bag inside. Blowing on the hot liquid, she took a sip and leaned her hip against the counter. "I spotted a bush that's growing some sort of new berries I've never seen at the far end of the meadow." She gestured toward the window above the sink. "Figured I'd pick them and test them to see if they're poisonous or if they could possibly help with the antidote formula I've been working on."

"I snooped around your lab yesterday," he said, flashing a grin. "You've done a great job rigging up a full-fledged science lab in the den of an abandoned farmhouse." He lifted his mug in a salute.

"We were lucky to find a house with so much vegetation nearby. I like trying different combinations and hope one of the teas I make will help Dani. Blueberries are known to strengthen memory, as well as kale and rosemary, which the previous owners planted in their garden. The teas don't taste that great, but hopefully, they're helping."

"She had a good day yesterday after I messed up," he said, swiping a hand over his face. "Even told me where to find her birthmark. Hopefully, today will be even better. You never know."

A throat cleared in the doorway, and their heads snapped toward Dani, who stood in the frame, knuckles white as she clutched a long metal candlestick in one hand. "I wouldn't be so sure, buddy," she muttered. "I'm assuming you're Maverick?" Lifting the phone, she shook it.

He gave a deep bow fit for the finest queen. "At your service, my lady."

"Hey, Dani," Raquel said with a soft smile.

"Hey," she said, gingerly approaching before setting the phone on the round dining table, although she held the candlestick firm. "Does the principal need to see you in the office?"

Maverick's lips curved at the inside phrase used between the sisters to signal something might be wrong. Dani used to save Raquel from having to participate in physical education class by showing up and telling the teacher the principal needed to see Raquel.

"Nope," Raquel said, shaking her head. "Everything's fine and we're not in danger. Promise."

Exhaling, Dani gingerly lowered the candlestick to the counter. "Holy shit. What the fuck is going on?"

Raquel approached her, and they shared a tight hug before Dani drew back and patted her side. "It seems like I destroyed the world, which I can't even begin to wrap my head around, and I have a huge fucking laceration on my side. What the hell?"

"Pitchfork accident about a week ago," Maverick interjected. "Raquel was with you when you fell."

"The sun was setting and you tripped and..." biting her lip, Raquel shrugged. "I mean, it wasn't funny, but it kind of was...until you got hurt and then I felt really bad. I lugged you back here, and Mav cleaned your wound."

Glancing at Maverick, Dani asked, "So, were your parents huge Tom Cruise fans? I'm not getting the name."

"Every fucking time," he muttered, rubbing his forehead as Raquel giggled. "I need you to get your memory back so we don't go through this every morning."

"Did I miss Mav getting 'Top Gunned'?" Arianna asked, striding into the kitchen.

"Barely," Raquel chimed.

"Shut it, you two," Maverick warned the sisters. "I'm going to make some breakfast and then I'll bring you up to speed, Dani. After that, Dominic and I need to head out and get more gas from that farm we scouted with all the tractors."

Their makeshift home had an abandoned pickup truck they were planning to drive to the Sendaxa lab in what was formerly Bethesda, Maryland, when they were ready to retrieve the antidote. Although Bethesda was now a ghost town since the wealthy had moved inside the fortified walls of Washington, DC, and the addicted had perished or relocated to one of the black-market compounds, the lab was still guarded by Sen Force soldiers. It was ground zero for the beginning of the world's downfall, and Sendaxa hadn't destroyed it...yet. But the knowledge the lab could be demolished—and any hope of retrieving Dani's secret antidote along with it—kept an urgency to their mission that couldn't be ignored.

"Will you go on foot?" Dani asked, lowering to one of the chairs at the dining table. "How far is it? Where the hell are we?"

"We're in an abandoned farmhouse in Waterford, Virginia, with a generator and a well, thank god. Dominic and I have been syphoning gas from nearby farms to make sure we have enough to drive to the lab once we're ready," Maverick said, striding over to her and lifting a tentative hand. Ever so gently, he placed it on her soft curls, thrilled when she didn't pull away. "Good morning, sweetheart," he said reverently.

Dani swallowed thickly, her eyes growing wide as she studied him, and Maverick dropped his hand, not wanting to push her or make her uncomfortable. Still, he missed touching her...missed the soft moans she expelled when he trailed kisses over the valley between her breasts...and the sexy purrs that escaped her pretty lips when he went lower...

Not wanting to be a creep, he strode back to the stove and pulled two pans from the cabinet. "Eggs as usual?" he asked, lifting his brows.

"Works for me," Arianna said, trailing to sit beside Dani before giving her a firm hug. Maverick heard her say softly, "He's a good one, sis. I wouldn't steer you wrong," to which Dani whispered, "Thank you," before releasing the embrace.

"No eggs for me," Raquel said, inching toward the back door. "Even in a world with limited food options, I can't seem to lose the baby weight." Her lips curved into a smile that didn't quite reach her eyes. "I'm going to go pick some of the wild raspberries."

"I'll go with you," Ari said, standing.

"No, it's fine," she said, turning the knob and opening the door. "They're on the far end of the yard by the tall evergreens, and still inside the perimeter you all built." Pointing toward the window above the sink, she added, "Mav can see me as he cooks."

Looking up from scrambling the eggs, which had been supplied by the chickens in the coop out back, Maverick squinted out the window. "I can barely see it, but yeah, I'll keep an eye out. Arianna scouted yesterday and everything was fine."

"About that," Arianna said as guilt clouded her features. "Something happened last night that I need to update you on."

"Is it a soldier thing?" Raquel asked. "If so, you can update me after my walk."

"That's fine," Arianna said. "I'll come find you after breakfast. I can tell you're itching to get outside. Go on."

"See you in a bit." With a wave, Raquel headed outside, closing the door behind her.

Maverick turned off the stove and scraped the eggs onto four plates in equal portions. He carried two to the table for Dani and Arianna before walking back and grabbing the two other plates. Dominic exited his bedroom that adjoined the kitchen, inhaling a deep breath.

"I smell eggs," he said in his deep baritone.

"Eat them while they're hot," Maverick said, gesturing to the seat next to him as he lowered into his own. "Arianna was about to give us an update."

A look passed between Arianna and Dominic.

"Before she starts, I'd like to say good morning, Dani," Dominic said. "I'm Dom and I'm part of the team. Hope the scar doesn't scare you. Arianna thinks it's hideous."

Arianna rolled her eyes as Dani glanced between Dominic and Maverick. "I have so many questions. Did I meet you at Sendaxa? I don't understand—"

"I'm going to answer them all for you," Maverick said, reaching over and squeezing her wrist. "But for now, let's just eat breakfast and pretend the world is normal for five minutes."

"Might as well update you while we eat," Arianna said gruffly. "I'll preface this by saying that my goal was to help some hungry kids. Unfortunately, things devolved..."

Arianna updated them while Dominic filled in some pieces along the way. Once she'd finished recounting the events of the previous night, she sat back and laced her fingers behind her head.

"So, that's it. Feel free to tell me how dumb it was to go out at night and possibly attract attention to our location."

"You wanted to bring some kids some food," Dani said, reaching over to squeeze her wrist. "I'd be pissed if you didn't help them, Ari. You couldn't have known a deserter would show up." She pursed her lips. "I'm going to need a briefing on what army he deserted from, but I assume one of you will catch me up."

"I will," Maverick said with a nod. "We'll take a walk after breakfast and I'll explain everything."

"Arianna and I will head out to examine the site," Dominic said. "The disappearance of the body is alarming, and we want to figure out who took it. But it's also pointless to worry about something we can't change."

Dani ate a forkful of eggs before asking, "Whose idea was it to make the video? That definitely helped when I woke up in a strange room with no memory."

"Yours," Maverick said, grinning. "We'd had a good day, and you wanted to ensure we had more of them."

"What does a good day entail?" she asked, her green eyes lit with curiosity.

"It means Mav gets laid," Arianna muttered.

"Jesus, Ari," Dominic interjected.

"Well, it's true." Wooden legs scraped the floor as she abruptly stood and carried her empty plate to the sink. "I'm going to go make sure the area around Raquel is safe and then we can head back to the site. Dani, do you want me to examine your side first or are you okay if Mav does it?" She pointed between Maverick and Dani.

"I..." Dani said hesitantly. "I guess it's okay if Maverick looks at it."

Arianna nodded before heading through the back door and closing it firmly behind her.

"Still the same Ari," Dani said, her gaze filled with wonder. "I'd be more weirded out if she and Raquel weren't here. For now, I'm just...overwhelmed."

Maverick smiled as admiration covered his features. "You're getting better each day at accepting the situation. I think you're building some muscle memory, even if you don't physically remember." He tapped his temple.

Dani remained silent, studying him as she often did each morning.

Maverick rose, collecting the dishes and washing them as he prepared himself for his daily briefing to his wife.

Chapter 6

After breakfast, Dani followed the incredibly handsome man who looked like the result of a baby between Timothy Olyphant and Patrick Dempsey into the living room. Forget Dr. McDreamy. Somehow, she'd woken up and the hottest silver fox in the world claimed to be her husband.

It would be cool if she hadn't destroyed humanity.

Which she was pretty sure she'd done, even though that certainly hadn't been her intention.

Man, life was a bitch sometimes.

"You okay?" Maverick asked, gesturing toward the weathered red plaid couch. "It was here when we found the house and it's ugly but comfortable."

Nodding, Dani sat, stiffening a bit when he lowered beside her.

"Don't worry," he said, the curving of his lips causing slight dimples to form under cheeks covered with a light smattering of black and gray stubble. "I'm not going to bite."

That's a shame...

The words flashed through her head before she cleared her throat and reminded herself she'd never seen this man in her life...but he and her sisters claimed he was her *husband*. Since it was too surreal to process, she glanced at her side.

"Soooo...do you want to treat my...pitchfork accident?" Scrunching her features, she said, "Wow. Those are two words I never thought I'd say together."

Chuckling, he rose and lifted a finger. "Be right back. Need to grab a wet cloth, fresh bandage and some of the antibiotic ointment the previous residents stocked in the upstairs bathroom cabinet. It's expired, but you and Raquel say it's better than nothing."

"Antibacterial cream is usually good years after expiration," she affirmed. "Should I...uh...take off my shirt?"

He cocked a brow. "Honestly, yeah, that will make it easier. Wait until I get back since you're not wearing a bra. I'll grab you one from your bedroom on the way."

"How do you know I'm not wearing a bra?"

"You never sleep in a bra, babe. Be right back."

Glancing down, she admitted he was right while simultaneously wondering who'd dressed her in the black tank top and boxer shorts. Had she dressed herself or had he done it? Shivering at the thought, she gnawed her lip while she awaited his return.

He returned, extending a hand with a functional beige bra hanging from one finger. Frowning, Dani grabbed it and stood. "Turn around," she said.

He breathed a laugh before turning and setting the supplies on the side table while she chucked her shirt and put on the bra. Once it was secure, she said, "Okay, ready."

"It's best if you lie on your back with your injured side facing me."

Dani's eyes darted between his as breath lodged in her throat.

"I won't try anything, Dani. Not really my style. If you want me to touch you, you'll ask. Come on. Let's get it done so we can head outside and I can brief you."

Feeling her heart thunk in her chest, she lay down on the couch.

"Lift your arm above your head," Maverick gently commanded, sending a jolt of pure arousal through her veins. Cognizant of the rising and falling of her chest, she lifted her arm, resting it beside her head.

Lowering, he sat beside her, his face a mask of concentration as he touched his fingers to the area where her skin met the adhesive tape. Dani sucked in a breath, and his striking eyes lifted to hers. "Are my fingers cold?"

Unable to speak, she shook her head, and he blinked before lowering his gaze to the bandage. His fingers scraped at the white gauze, gently tugging until he drew the bandage from her body. Studying the wound, he gently pushed the red skin surrounding the three circular punctures.

"Does that hurt?"

"It's tender, but it's not too bad," she rasped, wondering when someone had dropped a bag of gravel down her throat.

"Okay. I'll clean it, apply the ointment and put on a new bandage. I think we'll only need to do this two or three more times and it will be healed enough you won't need me to clean it for you."

Bummer. She'd have to give up having Silver Fox Hottie touch her while she lay sprawled on the couch? Was there another pitchfork she could walk into? Where was a random pitchfork when a girl needed one?

Maverick's lips pursed as mirth entered his eyes. "Were you just wondering if there's another pitchfork lying around you could fall into?"

Laughter bounded from her throat. "Yep. Busted."

His warm chuckle washed over her as he lifted the wet cloth and began to clean her wound. "Your sense of humor is what I noticed first, and it's killer. I couldn't believe a world-renowned geneticist could be so damn funny."

"How did we meet?"

"Sendaxa recruited you to develop EverLife and I was head of security at your lab. You worked a lot, which meant we spent a lot of time together."

"And you couldn't resist my dazzling knowledge of mitochondrial DNA?"

White teeth flashed as he grinned. "That and...other things." He slid the cloth over her skin one more time before setting it on the table and picking up the ointment. As he spoke, he spread the smooth gel over her wound. "You were so damn funny, and so determined to succeed. Every time you created a formula that failed, you'd pour yourself a glass of champagne and toast to another fantastic failure."

"I'm a huge fan of failure," she said, watching his fingers as they worked. "It's the only path to success."

"One of your favorite sayings," he confirmed with a nod. "Eventually, you roped me into having a sip of champagne with you here and there. It was so refreshing to meet someone who embraced failure. I'd never really contemplated having a positive attitude toward failing, and you were always so cute as we drank together."

"I'm sure Sendaxa wasn't happy their star scientist and head of security were drinking on the job."

"They never knew," he said, arching a mischievous eyebrow. "What use would I have been if I hadn't known how to hide from their cameras?"

"Indeed," she said, biting her lip. "But sharing stolen champagne is a long way from marriage. I'm exceedingly curious how that happened."

Remaining silent, he wiped his fingers on the wet cloth before picking up the large bandage. Removing the adhesive covering, he pressed the white gauze to her skin before patting the sides to ensure the adhesive stuck to her skin. After several firm presses, he straightened and ran his fingers over the bandage, causing her to shiver. "I think it's set," he said softly.

"Did I say something wrong?"

Those deep eyes lifted to hers. "No," he murmured, running a hand over his face. "It just makes me sad that you don't remember."

Dani's eyes widened as she studied him, something welling in her chest that felt a lot like...*remorse?*

"I'm sorry—"

"It's okay," he interjected, shaking his head. "One day you're going to remember, and it's going to be the happiest day of my damn life."

Slowly rising, she sat on the edge of the couch, wondering why she didn't feel more vulnerable in front of this man who was essentially a stranger. Here she was, clad in only a bra and boxer shorts, completely exposed. She should've felt trapped. Wary. Afraid. Instead, she felt drawn to the man whose face was now a mask of sadness and longing.

"Then tell me," she whispered, lifting her hand to gently rest her palm on his stubbled cheek. "Tell me how we fell in love. I'd really like to hear the story."

Emotion flared in his eyes as he smiled. "I promise, I'll tell you the story later. For now, I want to brief you. There's an urgency to our mission, and I have a feeling last night's events will only add to it. I've got work to do, but I don't want to leave you hanging." Rising, he extended his hand. "Come on, slugger. Let's get to it."

Chapter 7

After throwing on a t-shirt and sneakers, Dani headed outside with Maverick, taking in the expansive meadows and forests that surrounded the farmhouse. "Who lived here before?"

"We don't know," he said, shaking his head as he walked beside her. "Once they locked down the cities and medical care became scarce outside the city walls, people began to migrate toward the black-market compounds. Many left their lives and belongings behind, only concerned with finding more EverLife. Whoever owned this farm was long gone before we arrived."

"How do you know?"

"The food in the fridge and on the counter was rotted, and there was a severe ant problem, which Raquel insisted on eradicating." He flashed a grin. "Waterford is far enough off the grid, and this place is remote enough that Dom, Arianna and I decided to set a temporary base here."

"How long ago?"

"We've been here for three months."

A heavy rush of air escaped her lungs. "I lost my memory three months ago," she said flatly. "After I created a drug that hurt so many." Halting, she turned to face him, the sun burning her eyes as they welled. "How many people have died?"

"Don't do this to yourself, sweetheart," he said, gently rubbing her upper arm. "No one could've foreseen this—"

"I should've foreseen it," she said, angrily swiping the tear that escaped and trailed down her cheek. "I should be arrested and tried for murder. It's no less than I deserve."

His nostrils flared as he inhaled a deep breath, the smooth strokes of his palm against the skin of her upper arm soothing. "We can't turn you in. We need you, Dani. You're going to remember the code, and we're going to break into the lab so we can fix this."

"I just want to help people," she whispered, her throat bobbing as it burned with clogged emotion. "To cure cancer so people won't suffer like we did with Mom. That's what I was working on at Columbia. How did I fuck everything up so badly?"

"Your intentions were good, sweetheart." Stepping forward, he drew her close, aligning their bodies, the firm ridges of his chest and thighs pressing into hers. "Sendaxa promised they'd fund your cancer vaccine research once you finished EverLife. Sometimes shit happens even when we try our best and have good intentions."

Her throat bobbed as she stared deep into his eyes, smoldering with love and compassion. "I have to fix it," she said softly.

"We will. That's what we're doing here. We're working our way up to breaking into the lab to steal the secret stash of antidote you hid before you lost your memory. Once we have that, you and Raquel can replicate it, mass produce it, and we can begin to distribute it to the black-market compounds."

Dani mulled the plan over in her head, both overwhelmingly complex and simple at once. "It's a lot for a five-person team to take on, especially when you have to spend hours explaining the situation to me every day."

Huffing a laugh, he nodded. "It would be easier if we could cut the daily recaps. I haven't figured out how yet. The video helps, but you're still wary until we have a chance to talk like we are now."

Dani's eyes lowered, roving over the neckline of his t-shirt and the tiny black and gray hairs that sprung around the collar. How many times had she trailed her fingers through them? How many times had she made love with this stranger who spoke to her with such familiar reverence? Lifting her hand, she placed it over his heart, strangely comforted by the firm beats beneath her palm.

Maverick's eyes closed as he seemed to melt underneath her touch. A muscle ticked in his jaw, the strong muscles of his neck chording as he allowed her to explore. Sliding her hand to his collar, she delved her fingers inside, brushing the backs against the prickly hairs. A low groan escaped his throat, causing her body to inflame.

"Babe," he rasped, his breath choppy as he squeezed his eyelids together. "I want you to touch me...*everywhere*...believe me." Lifting his lids, his gaze drilled into hers. "But Dom and I have to go retrieve some gas today, so I need to finish our briefing and get on the road."

"Okay," she whispered, aware of the swirling emotions deep in her gut. Guilt she'd hurt so many people. Remorse she couldn't bring back the ones that were already lost. Determination to save those who still had a chance. Desire for the man who seemed intent on helping her accomplish that task. "Have I tried keeping a journal? What methods have I tried to condense this daily process?"

"You do have a notebook where you write things down, but in the end, it's always easier for us to talk." Grasping her hand, he brought it to his lips, gently kissing her palm. "You don't remember me here when you wake up," he tapped her forehead, "but your body remembers me. Your hands remember me." He placed another reverent kiss before lowering her hand and releasing it. Dani flexed her fingers, already missing his touch. "So, it was just easier to do this every morning"—he circled his hand between them—"than for you to spend an hour reading a journal."

Lowering her gaze, she stared at the spongy grass as she gnawed her lip, pondering how to jog her memory so they could escape this nightmare and enter the next phase of their plan. Cementing her gaze to his, she said, "We have to find a solution. Three months is too long. We can't remain inactive, especially if bodies are mysteriously disappearing."

"I agree," he confirmed, gently brushing away the hair that blew across her cheek. "If you don't recover your memory soon, we're going to just break into the lab and try to blow the locks to bits so we can retrieve the antidote. You armed the door to the secret storage unit with a ten-digit security code, which we hope you'll remember. If not, you'll still need to scan your fingerprint. Without the code, the chances of us breaching the lab, retrieving the antidote and escaping intact are slim, but we're going to try."

"You know the layout since you were head of security?"

"Yes, and Dom worked there too. We know it intimately."

Chewing the inside of her lip, Dani digested the information. "Okay. The lab is heavily guarded, I assume?"

"It is, but it's outside the city walls, which gives it a vulnerability it wouldn't have otherwise. Between Dom, Arianna and I, we think we can take the soldiers. Raquel isn't a soldier, so we'll retrieve her after the mission. Or she'll continue the mission if we fail."

"I don't want her left alone," Dani said, concern for her sister flaring in her chest.

"Then we'll have to succeed," he said firmly. "You're determined to save the world, and I've never met a more tenacious woman than you, sweetheart. Along with Arianna and Raquel. The Lawson sisters are fierce."

Sighing, she ran a hand through her hair. "I failed at helping people and created a huge disaster instead. I feel anything but fierce. It's unforgiveable."

"There's no point in dwelling on things we can't change, Dani," he said, sliding his fingers under her chin to stare deep into her eyes. "All we can do now is fix it."

"I'm ready," she whispered, straightening her spine. "Let's get fucking started."

Chuckling, he leaned down and brushed a kiss across her lips, his lips soft yet firm as they caressed hers.

"Sorry," he whispered, shaking his head. "You're just so cute when you get that determined glint in your eye. I couldn't resist."

"Will you tell me about our first kiss one day? I'd really like to know."

"Yeah." Dropping his hand, Dani shivered at the loss of his warm fingers against her chin. "How about when Dom and I get back tonight?"

"It's a date," she breathed, her voice raspy as they stood in the warm breeze, their bodies humming in tune even though they were no longer touching.

"Come on. Let's get you set up in Raquel's lab. You like to work with her on the various vegetation and tea combos. I think you're healed enough to work today."

Stepping back, he extended his hand and she took it, interlacing their fingers before he led her back to the house. He gave her a quick tour of the lab, which was impressive considering the lack of scientific equipment at the farmhouse, and kissed her once more on the forehead before he headed outside to wait for Dominic and Arianna to return.

Staring at the various concoctions and the vegetation spread across the large table, Dani grabbed the nearby notebook that had her scrawled notes and got to work.

Chapter 8

Dominic returned from scouting the campsite, annoyed he and Arianna found no clues of who moved the deserter's body. After heading to his room and fishing a pesky rock from his boot, he slipped it back on and stood from the rickety bed. It was better than sleeping on the floor, so he wouldn't complain, but a part of him detested the fact the Sendaxa executives and their supporters slept in luxury every night. Safe in their walled-off cities, they'd left the destruction of society behind, carelessly hoarding all available EverLife and the antidote supplies and shutting out the rest of the world.

They were a bunch of bastards, and Dominic couldn't wait to bring them down.

The odds against him and the rest of their scrappy team were vast, but Dominic knew they'd do their best to accomplish their goal or die trying. There was honor in that, and it was extremely important to Dominic to live with honor since so many others had lost their chance.

The image of his parents and sister flashed through his mind, causing him to smile as he rested his palms flat on the dresser. He stared into his withered face and dark brown eyes, remembering how his sister, Pam, used to tease him after he'd sustained the scar that now marred his features.

He'd been deployed on a special ops mission back when he was still a Navy Seal. A young man who'd believed in optimistic ideals like democracy and freedom. His team was tasked with taking out a high-level operative in a terrorist regime in Pakistan. It wasn't his first mission designed to target and assassinate a threat, but it would end up being the deadliest.

Somehow, the terrorist cell and their leader had known about the impending attack. Dominic's team of twelve men charged into an ambush and only three survived. A rebel soldier had pulled a machete from his belt, slashing it across Dominic's face before he regained his wits enough to shoot a spray of bullets from his rifle into the man's chest. Dominic could still remember the blood dripping from his nose and cheeks as his commander gripped his arm and tugged him out of the cave into the dark night. Dominic returned home with his commander and one fellow comrade, their bodies bludgeoned and their spirits broken.

Dominic's parents and sister had taken him in, nursing him back to health after he was honorably discharged from duty. In those days after his release from the hospital, Pam would tiptoe into the room and leave snacks for him on the bedside table. Sometimes, she brought him ice cream, and they ate together as she teased him about his scar. She'd tell him he needed to create an online dating profile specifically looking for girls who dug scars and wounded men.

His nineteen-year-old sister had been wise, even though she was five years his junior. She would always gently remind him that he'd lived when others hadn't, and he had a duty to attempt to thrive. So, Dominic had reentered the world, picking up various short-term security jobs as he struggled with PTSD. Pam urged him to see a therapist, and the bi-monthly visits with Dr. Langone helped as he slowly began to rebuild his life.

And then, he came home one evening to find his parents dead in their Washington, DC townhome. Although their Adams Morgan neighborhood was relatively safe, Dominic had later learned the burglars had followed his parents home. The attack had been calculated, and when the criminals forced themselves inside, his parents hadn't stood a chance. The two men shot them dead before absconding with his mother's jewelry and his dad's wallet, taken from his lifeless body.

Dominic had been at a PTSD recovery meeting, and Pam had been at study group at George Washington University, where she was a sophomore. She'd returned home to find their living room swarming with cops and EMTs. They'd held each other as members of the coroner's office wheeled away their parents' bodies, unable to comprehend the loss. Three weeks later, the two burglars were apprehended and eventually put on trial, where they were both sentenced to life in prison.

It all seemed so senseless to Dominic, who'd lost most of his team in Pakistan only to return and lose his parents a year later.

And then, as Dominic and Pam began to settle their parents' estate, she began to feel sick. He urged her to go to the doctor, but she brushed him off, saying it was something she ate or allergies. "I'm twenty, bro," she'd say with a cheeky grin. "Healthy as a horse. I don't want you worrying about me."

As her sophomore year wound down and she began to lose weight, Dominic threatened to carry her to the doctor's office if she didn't make time for a checkup. She'd stared at him with eyes the color of his own, with dark circles underneath that had only recently appeared, and finally agreed to a physical.

The cancer diagnosis came several weeks later. Lung cancer, although she'd never smoked a day in her life and was a few months shy of twenty-one years old. A crushing diagnosis that was already in Stage 4 when discovered. She withdrew from school to focus on her health—and the various chemo, radiation and drug therapies—before her body began to truly break down several months later.

Living in the home where his parents were murdered, Dominic nursed his dying sister until he accepted the inevitable. Hospice was brought in, and he sat by her bedside every night, holding her hand as he tried to memorize everything about his last living blood relative.

"You've had so much pain," Pam rasped one night, coughing as she lay on the cool sheets. Bones jutted from her thin, cancer-ridden body and the smell of death pervaded the room even though she continued to smile through the agony. "And now I'm going to leave you too, and I'm afraid you're never going to allow yourself to love again."

Dominic studied her, wishing he could promise her he would but unable to utter the words. What was the point of connecting with people—of having a family—only to live with the knowledge they could be ripped away at any time? The thought of caring for someone else and reliving the intense pain he felt as he gazed into his sister's eyes, dull from pain medication, made him cringe. It was something he couldn't possibly fathom in the moment. Perhaps never again. Time was a powerful healer but only for those who wished to be healed.

Dominic was quite sure he'd lost that desire. He wasn't sure where that left him, but it most likely led to a lonely life working dead-end security jobs until he met his maker. Still, being lonely was better than the terrible suffering he'd experienced in his two and a half decades on the planet, so he accepted that fate as the preferable alternative.

Until he'd met Dr. Danica Lawson.

Over a decade later, Dominic was in between security jobs when a buddy told him about an opening at Sendaxa. The pharmaceutical-biotech company was working on a new drug in their fancy lab at the facility in Bethesda. They wanted experienced security specialists who could work long shifts for abnormal hours since the scientists were on a deadline to create a new drug to satisfy investors.

After his first interview with Maverick Ward, Dominic knew it was a job at which he would excel. He liked Maverick, who was also former military, and he was offered the job after two more rounds of interviews and various background checks. Dominic had sold his parents' townhome years before, so he ended his lease on his apartment in Washington, DC and relocated to a one-bedroom unit in Bethesda.

"Before the world went to shit," Dominic murmured to his reflection. Pushing away the morbid thoughts, he secured the holster on his belt before exiting his room and heading toward the makeshift lab where Raquel and Dani often worked.

Striding up to the open doorframe, Dominic leaned against it, grinning as he observed Dani sitting at the lab table scrawling in a notebook. Her tongue was situated between her teeth as she wrote out some equation he'd never understand, tossing him back into his memories.

He'd first seen her like this—in her element clad in a white lab coat—at the sterile lab at Sendaxa. The lab was a marvel of technology, complete with every modern upgrade Dani would need to create EverLife and make the company billions. As she'd worked, lifting a dropper to dispense something onto a Petri dish, she must've sensed his presence. Her green eyes latched onto his and widened as she gasped.

"Holy shit," she whispered, lowering the dropper and dish and placing her hand over her heart. "You scared me. You must be the new security guard. Maverick told me you'd be starting today."

"I am." Stepping into the lab, he walked forward until a few feet separated them. "I'm very sorry to scare you, ma'am. I'm Dominic Cavalleri, and I asked Mr. Ward to tell you about the scar." He pointed at his face, understanding that seeing the ugly wound was usually a shock for people.

"Oh, he did," she said, waving her hand, "and it's not that bad. We all have scars, right? Some are just on the inside where people can't see."

"True," he said, feeling his lips curve at her kindness. "Well, it's nice to meet you, Dr. Lawson." He extended his hand.

"Oh, please call me Dani. Everyone does." They shook as Dominic felt an undeniable spark in his chest. He would later realize the flare was emotion—something he hadn't allowed himself to feel in so long. But he'd felt it for the lovely woman who accepted him, scars and all, from the first day they met.

Returning to the moment, Dominic cleared his throat so he wouldn't startle her as she worked at the makeshift farmhouse lab.

"Oh...hello, Dominic," Dani said, lifting her head from the notebook, curiosity in her eyes. "I think Maverick was looking for you."

"He's getting ready and then we're heading out." Tentatively striding forward, he pointed at the notebook. "Any science miracles happening here today?"

"Well, I just got started," she said, chewing on the pen cap as she flipped through the notebook, "but Raquel has some great notes here, and I've left some too. I can tell since my handwriting is ten times worse than hers." Smiling, she tilted her head. "Guess I'm not in the twilight zone after all. I'm just an amnesia survivor who needs to get her memory back."

"I'd say our reality is way stranger than the twilight zone, but that's just my take" was his sardonic reply as he cocked a brow. "But it's still exciting, I guess."

She studied him as she often did each day after she woke up and met him for the "first" time. After a few moments, she asked, "Were we good friends? Before the world fell apart?"

Nodding, he closed the distance between them, leaning his hip on the table as he crossed his arms over his chest. "We were. You worked all the time and liked to chat while you worked. Since Mav and I were the only ones there with you most of the time, depending on what shifts we were working, you talked to us a lot."

Her eyebrows lifted as she flashed a cheeky grin. "Maverick says I forced him to drink champagne with me and that's how we fell in love. What did you and I bond over? I didn't make you smoke a joint with me, did I?"

Laughter sprung from his throat as he shook his head. "No, but that would've been fun." Tracing the wooden lab table with his finger, he cleared his throat. "You told me about your mom...and my sister also died of cancer. We eventually bonded over the shared experiences and...comforted each other, I guess you could say."

"Oh, Dominic," she said, rising and placing her hand on his bicep. Squeezing, she gazed up at him, empathy shining in her eyes. "I'm so sorry. She must've been young."

"Twenty-one years old," he said, his voice raspy. "My parents died the year before and then she passed. It was quite overwhelming. Years later, I met you." Lifting his hand, he cupped her shoulder, returning her comforting gesture. "Talking about it with someone else who had been through it was cathartic."

"I'm sure it was for me too. Watching my mom die from cancer is the entire reason I wanted to create a cure. I knew if I worked hard enough and secured funding, I could create a vaccine so no one else would have to suffer like that."

"You still can, Dani." His fingers dug into her shoulder, gentle but sure. "We've just got to help those affected by EverLife first. And then, I promise you, we're going to ensure you create your cancer vaccine."

"Thank you," she whispered, tears welling along her lashes.

"Okay, buddy, hands where I can see them," Maverick teased, striding into the room. "Ready to syphon some gas?"

"Ready," Dominic said, dropping his hand. Maverick was his best friend and cool as fuck regarding the fact that Dominic was in love with his wife, but he didn't want to push it. After all, his feelings for Dani could never go anywhere, and Dominic was perfectly fine with that.

Loving Dani wasn't about reality. He'd given up on experiencing any form of real emotion after his parents and sister died. No, loving her was an...*idea* more than anything. A way for him to connect with someone who'd had a similar experience without any possibility of actually having to put himself out there.

Dani would always belong to Maverick, which meant she was safe. Loving her would never hurt. It would offer comfort but allow him to keep the wall he'd built around his heart intact. After the crushing agony he'd experienced from his family's death, it was the only way he knew how to process emotion.

So, he loved her from afar, thankful to every god in the universe she loved someone else.

It might have seemed a sad tale to someone else, but Dominic rarely gave a shit what others thought. Loving

Dani these past few years had led to a healing, of sorts, if not all the way, and that in itself was a small miracle he would allow himself to enjoy.

"Dom?" Maverick called, gesturing him toward the kitchen. "Let's go."

Sending an affable salute to Dani, he followed her husband so they could complete the day's mission.

CHAPTER 9

M averick and Dominic began the trek across the fields, careful to walk through wooded areas when possible. Although they were in a remote area, they both understood the importance of remaining inconspicuous.

As his boots crunched the grass, Maverick observed the evidence of destruction. Power lines that had once traversed the countryside were now strewn across the fields. Some of the utility poles were charred, perhaps from addicts who'd camped out and used them to build fires. Others were chopped into parts, some of the wood carried off by people who could use it to build makeshift encampments or bonfires.

Entering an area with a dirt path, they hiked as Maverick noticed the discarded syringes scattered along the trail. The surrounding trees would've created a hideout for addicts when the world began to fell apart. Now, it was empty. Anyone who'd camped here had long since moved on. Either to a black-market compound...or to meet their maker. Maverick's lips thinned at the somber thought.

When they exited the thicket, a tall metal tower greeted them. It was now a fossil in a world once dominated by cell phones and technology. It sat eerily under the glowing sun, rusting as the world adjusted to the new normal.

Maverick glanced at Dominic as they passed the tower. "You're quiet today, man," he said as they navigated through the uncut grass.

"I'm always quiet."

Huffing a laugh, he nodded. "True. But something's off today."

Dominic scowled as he harshly rubbed his forehead. "Bodies are disappearing, man. I'm afraid our cover's blown. I wanted to wait for Dani's memory to come back, but..."

"I know," Maverick softly replied. "We're going to have to initiate Phase II, whether we're ready or not. Since Dani can't remember the code, we're going to have to make a damn good plan."

"Agreed."

They strode in silence as they pondered the huge task before them. Finally, Dominic said, "We'll never succeed if Sendaxa decides to use military force outside the cities. Luthor Cromwell isn't going to accept us distributing the antidote to those who need it. If Sen Force begins attacking the compounds, people will die before we can save them."

"Do you really think they want a war?" Maverick asked, eyes narrowing as he considered the prospect. "Luthor has everything he wants. He controls all the remaining technology in the world and is the leader of the Sendaxa cities. Every former general and commander of the US military reports to him since he stepped in and took over the government when President Johnson overdosed on EverLife." He shook his head at the sadness and senselessness of the president's demise.

"Such a waste," Dominic murmured. "Wanting to stay alive forever, so you shove shit in your body that kills it. I'll just never understand it."

"I think it's just human nature," Maverick said, patting him on the shoulder.

"I guess." They approached the clearing where three tractors sat. Each were nearly full with gas, and both men would fill the empty containers attached to their packs, strap them back on and lug the gas back to the farmhouse. They'd decided not to chance driving during the day since a moving truck would draw attention and they needed to remain hidden.

Removing his pack, Dominic sat it on the ground and rubbed the back of his neck, massaging the tight muscles there. "I think I worry because men like Cromwell are never satisfied with getting everything they want. They always want more power until it eventually destroys them and everyone around them. Look at what happened when he decided to play God and create a drug that would double humans' lifespans." He snapped his fingers. "Up in flames, Mav. A guy with that ego isn't done yet, and he has limitless resources. I think it's only a matter of time before he begins to attack the black-market compounds."

"To what end?" Maverick asked, pulling the rubber hose with the pump he'd fashioned on the end out of his bag.

"To create a world in his image," Dominic said, shrugging. "A world where only the Sendaxa cities exist and everyone else is exterminated."

"Wow," Maverick said, shaking his head as he unscrewed the gas cap on the nearest tractor. "Did you read a lot of George Orwell and Stephen King as a kid? That's dark, man."

"I'm kind of a pessimist, in case you haven't noticed," he muttered, cocking a brow.

"Uh, yeah, I got the memo. Come on. Help me with this."

They began to syphon the gas, extending the tube into the tank and the other end into one of the eight containers they'd brought. Maverick had fashioned the tube with a bicycle pump he found in the garage, allowing them to pump the liquid. Once full, they would lace a rope through the handles of the containers, strap them on their backs, and carry them home.

As they worked, Maverick thought about the best possible outcome, if their plan actually succeeded.

First, Dani would have to replicate the antidote, and while they aligned with trustworthy people at the compounds, people who wouldn't be seduced by the lure of riches and technology that still existed in the walled-off Sendaxa cities.

Second, they'd need to find an abandoned warehouse or factory to produce enough quantities to distribute to all the people who so desperately needed it.

Third, they would need protection as they extended their reach across the country and eventually the globe. Sendaxa employed the Sen Force, which was essentially the former US military, and it made them formidable. The more Maverick thought about it, the more he realized they needed to begin recruiting soldiers. But where? Strung-out addicts from black-market compounds certainly wouldn't be ready for combat. They'd somehow need to recruit soldiers who weren't addicted to EverLife nor loyal to Sendaxa. No small feat in their current situation.

"We need to start building a militia," Dominic murmured, echoing his thoughts. "It's the only way we're going to have half a chance, Mav."

"I know," he said, working the pump. "We were so focused on regaining Dani's memory." He drifted off, tapping the hose against the full container before sliding it into the nearby empty one. "And, selfishly, I don't want her to get hurt. But she wants to save the world, and I've got to help her try."

"Even if our chances are close to zero."

Maverick's lips pursed. "You know, I think I liked you better when you weren't talking."

Laughing, he nodded. "You and Ari both. I think she tells me to shut up as much as I tell her."

Keeping his gaze averted in the hopes Dominic wouldn't feel interrogated, Maverick asked, "You ever think about her? In that way? Might take your mind off other things."

Dominic's hand froze as he was moving an empty container toward the one Maverick was rapidly filling. "Arianna?" he asked, stunned. "She hates me."

Maverick lifted a shoulder. "For someone who hates you, she exudes some palpable energy toward you, and you shoot it right back. It's impossible not to notice, man."

"Because she's a loner who hates that I want to help her. She's a skilled soldier and we need her, but I hate that she puts herself at risk when she tries to do everything alone."

Pausing, Maverick stared into his friend's eyes. "Sounds like you care about her and don't want her to get hurt."

With a *pfft*, Dominic sliced his hand through the air. "I'm just smart enough to realize we need her. And she's been very clear she thinks I'm an ugly jerk and she'd rather wrap herself around a frayed electrical wire before being anywhere near me."

"Maybe she just doesn't want to try with a man who's decided he wants someone else. She's got a lot of pride. It's a Lawson family trait."

Dominic remained silent, digesting Maverick's words as he finished filling the gas. Once all the containers were full, they carefully tied them to their packs and strapped them on their shoulders, ready to head back.

Something snapped in the distance, and their heads swung toward the nearby forest before they locked gazes.

"Gun cocking," Maverick said softly.

"Confirmed," Dominic replied.

With confident nods, they each dropped their heavy, gas-laden packs to the ground and drew their guns, aiming them at the forest. Another click sounded and Maverick commanded, "Take cover."

Maneuvering behind the tractors, they crouched, each lifting their arms to rest on the green metal of the tractors and aimed into the woods.

"Show yourself!" Maverick shouted. "We're armed and ready to fight!"

A man stepped from the forest, tall and toned, the bronzed skin of his arms glistening in the afternoon sunlight. Five men followed behind him, and he held up a fist, commanding them to halt.

"Well, boys, looks like it's six against two," the man said, his tone slightly ominous. "I like those odds, but we're not here to harm you."

Glancing at Dominic, Maverick felt his chest swell at his friend's affirmative nod, indicating he was willing to fight the six men, just the two of them. Straightening, Maverick cocked his gun and tilted his head. "The rifles slung over your shoulders would suggest otherwise. Bring it on, motherfucker. We'll fight you all day long."

The leader still held his fist high, but the men behind him disobeyed the order, lifting their guns. Maverick and Dominic spared each other one last glance before opening fire.

In an instant, the soft chirp of birds gave way to the sounds of bullets being sprayed across the dry, uneven grass as all hell broke loose.

Chapter 10

Dominic heard the bullet whiz past his ear as he crouched behind the tractor. Rising, he fired a few precise shots, elation coursing through him when one of the men fell. One down, five to go. Glancing over at Maverick, he jerked his head toward the men, indicating they should begin to advance. Maverick gave a curt nod, and they slowly edged toward the side of their respective tractors.

Maverick straightened and shot one of the attackers directly between his dark eyebrows. The soldier's eyes widened before he expelled his last breath and crumbled to the ground. Dominic's boots crunched the grass as he continued the advance, thankful to get a clean shot in one of the men's necks. Groaning in pain, the soldier fell as the leader glared at him in frustration. Lifting his hand, the leader halted the fighting.

"Enough," he said, slowly lifting his rifle before slinging it behind his shoulder. "I meant it when I said I didn't want to shoot you." Glancing at the fallen men, he shook his head. "Such a waste. They shouldn't have raised their weapons."

Dominic's eyes narrowed as he clutched his gun, still holding it high as he aimed it between the leader's eyes. The injured soldier lay on the ground, writhing in pain as he cupped his bleeding neck. Glancing toward him, the leader sighed and lifted a handgun from his belt. Aiming it at his comrade as he wiggled on the ground, he shot him directly in the temple. The soldier gasped, his body stiffening, before his muscles lost their rigidity and he melted against the ground.

"Jesus, man," Maverick said, still holding his gun high. "You killed your own soldier."

"He was suffering and never going to make it," the leader said, his tone unwavering. "I did him a favor. And it's Tristan. Tristan Holder."

"Sir, we should retreat," the remaining soldier said, his expression wary as he contemplated Maverick and Dominic.

"Go back to the jeep and wait for me," Tristan said, gesturing with his head toward the woods. "I want to talk to these two alone. I'll be there in five minutes, and we'll head back to the Sendaxa District."

The soldier spared Maverick and Dominic one last cautious glare before pivoting and striding into the woods.

"You can put away the guns," Tristan said, holstering his handgun and resting his hands on his hips above camouflage pants. "I have no desire to kill you."

"Hard to believe since you just opened fire on us," Dominic muttered.

"Do you work for Sendaxa?" Maverick asked. "Are you on the Sen Force?"

Tristan squinted one eye. "I'm more of a...mercenary you could say. I do the dirty stuff Luthor Cromwell doesn't want to claim."

"He's already pretty dirty," Dominic said acerbically. "His drug eliminated over half the world's population and destroyed society as we know it."

"True, but he still longs to maintain a cultured appearance. Most men with overgrown egos do. It's important his wealthy friends see him as a savior instead of a savage. Sometimes the line between them is very thin." He held his thumb and forefinger an inch apart.

"Did you remove the body from the campsite last night?" Dominic asked.

"Yes. Bodies are valuable in today's world, especially ones that are barely cold." Tristan's lips thinned. "I sold it to a group of dealers on their way to a black-market site in West Virginia. They paid well."

Disgust coiled in Dominic's stomach. Food was scarce in some of the more derelict compounds, and he'd heard rumors that some had resorted to extremes in order to survive. Still, he didn't want to believe people had sunk so low they would turn cannibalistic.

"Are you telling me they...?" Maverick's voice drifted off.

"I don't give a shit what they did with the body," Tristan said, showing his palms. "I just wanted the money."

"Why?" Dominic asked. "You just told us you work for Luthor Cromwell."

"He *thinks* I work for him. But things aren't always as they appear. I need money because I have my own plans."

Gazing over his shoulder, Tristan pointed in the direction of the farmhouse. "Cromwell knows you're here. His soldiers discovered your location last week, but he hasn't given the order to kill Dr. Lawson...yet"—he arched an ominous brow—"because he has other plans for her."

Stiffening, Maverick's jaw clenched so tight Dominic thought it might snap off his face. "No one is laying a finger on my wife, asshole. Got it?"

"I have no desire to harm her," he said, showing his palms. "But Cromwell is drunk with power and sees her as the key to gaining more."

"How? She'll never work for him again. She wants to heal people, not harm them."

Tristan cocked a brow. "Let's just say Cromwell thinks he's smarter than everyone, but I'm betting your scrappy little team might just best him."

Maverick and Dominic shared a glance as the tension thickened.

"Even though I've been given refuge inside the District, it's not a safe place for vagrants like me," Tristan continued. "There's an underlying current of realization that's rapidly dawning: the rich are safe and the rest are expendable."

"How so?" Dominic asked.

"The wealthy cronies who made it into the District don't know how to exist without their servants, yachts and opulence. They've begun to call for the middle-class residents to take up laborers' jobs. House cleaning, cooking, child care. All the shit the uber-wealthy don't want to do. Regular people thought they'd be accepted by the elite, but they're starting to realize it was a pipe dream."

"So the addicted and homeless suffer outside the walls, and half the people inside the walls realize life was better before society fell." Maverick shifted his weight, placing a fist on his hip as he contemplated. Finally, he said, "There's going to be a rebellion."

"Maybe," Tristan said, lifting a shoulder. "Most people I've met in the District aren't *that* impressive...but there's hope."

Maverick studied him. "So, what's your objective? You don't seem like Cromwell's biggest fan."

A muscle ticked in Tristan's jaw. "I'm not, but staying close to him gives me access I need to put my own plans in motion. And before you ask me what they are, I'll kindly tell you they're none of your business."

Maverick and Dominic remained silent, understanding they weren't getting more information from the mysterious man.

"I have a map saved in here of all the black-market compounds," Tristan said, lifting a smart phone from his belt and shaking the device. "I'll share it with you once you break into the lab and retrieve the antidote. Some compounds have smart, capable leaders who've controlled the rampant addition within their walls. I'd start with those if you want any chance of success."

"Are you always this bossy?" Dominic muttered.

Ignoring him, Tristan continued. "If you're lucky, I might even leave some weapons for you in the shed to increase your chance of success."

Exasperated, Maverick extended his hands at his sides. "What's in this for you? I don't understand your motives."

Tristan's eyes shone under the late afternoon sunlight as he studied them. "There are many things in play here you don't understand." He held up a finger when Maverick opened his mouth to argue. "But it's time to break into the lab. The clock is ticking and Cromwell isn't stable." He began slowly easing back into the woods.

"Wait!" Maverick called, stalking forward before Tristan slung his rifle around and aimed it at him.

"That's far enough," Tristan warned, continuing his retreat. "Get the gas back home and make a plan with your team so my comrade and I can bury these soldiers." He gestured with his head toward the slain bodies. "Each day you wait, the odds stack more against you. Stop wasting time." With a salute, he turned and stalked into the forest.

"What the fuck?" Dominic breathed.

"Tristan Holder," Maverick said, tapping his forehead. "We need to ask Arianna if she ever heard the name during her time in the military. Maybe she can shed some light on him."

Glancing back at the gas containers, Dominic nodded. "Let's get the fuck out of here. I don't like being exposed, or the fact that bastard snuck up on us."

"Heard," Maverick said, patting him on the shoulder.

They strapped the containers on their backs once again and marched across the field under the late afternoon sun.

CHAPTER 11

D ani sat on the uncomfortable stool, absently shifting her weight as she leaned over the notebook. She'd written pages of meticulous notes, mostly with chemical equations that could possibly lead to an antidote for Ever-Life. There were other notes too, about different herbs and teas Raquel had mixed to try and regenerate her memory, as well as random notes that didn't make much sense at all.

In several places, Dani had written various Latin phrases. She'd always loved Latin, and very few people understood it, so she sometimes thought of it as a secret language all for herself. Silly since entire civilizations had spoken it in the past, but they were long gone and it always gave her a tiny thrill whenever she observed the language being used in modern society.

Running her finger over the Latin scrawling, she read aloud—quietly since Arianna and Raquel were preparing dinner in the kitchen. Arianna had stayed back to keep watch while Maverick and Dominic traveled to syphon the gas, and having her sisters nearby comforted Dani.

Many of the Latin phrases she'd written were well known and quite inspirational.

- *Acta non verba* (deeds, not words)

- *Audentes fortuna iuvat* (fortune favors the bold)

- *Aut viam inveniam aut faciam* (I will find a way or make one)

But there were others as she read further, each becoming more ominous as she scrolled down with her finger.

- *Fere libenter homines id quod volunt credunt* (Men generally believe what they want to)

- *Nemo mortalium omnibus horis sapit* (Of mortal men, none is wise at all times)

- *De omnibus dubitandum* (Be suspicious of everything)

And finally, at the very end, *et tu, Brute?*, which was one of the most commonly known Latin phrases, even by those who didn't speak it. A phrase that expressed Julius Caesar's shock at the discovery his friend Brutus conspired to murder him. Narrowing her eyes, she focused on the missives.

"What were you trying to say here, Dani?" she asked, frustrated her memory was a pit of blackness. Closing her eyes, she squeezed her lids tight, trying to remember something...*anything* after her last memory all those years ago when she lived in New York and worked as a professor at the genetics department at Columbia University.

Settling into the darkness, she allowed the puffs of light to creep into the corners of her vision, almost like smoke billowing from the recesses of her subconscious. Resting her forehead on her hands, her elbows dug into the table as she concentrated.

Echoes of metal clicking ticked in the background, and Dani saw her own hands, unlatching a steel door with biomedical warning symbols. Pulling it open, she reached inside, ready to grasp the contents before she felt the presence behind her. Gasping, she turned, unprepared for the explosion of pain in her skull as someone struck her...

"Dani?" Raquel asked, causing her to flinch and place her hand over her rapidly beating heart. "Are you okay?"

"Shit," Dani whispered, shaking her head. "I think I just had a flashback...possibly to the few moments before encountering the person who did this to me." Reaching toward the base of her head, she rubbed the area that covered her hippocampus. As a scientist, she knew that was the region that had been injured when she'd been struck. It was responsible for episodic and connected memories.

"That's amazing, Dani," Raquel said, squeezing her shoulder. "Every once and a while you have a flashback, but it only lasts a few seconds and you don't remember it when you wake up the next day."

"Which is something I have to change." Straightening, she pointed at the notebook. "I've been writing random notes in here, but we both know nothing I do is random."

"Truth," her sister said, grinning. "Your brain is always leaving clues behind. It gives me hope you're going to see something you scribbled down and it will jog your memory. I think once you cross the threshold of having full-on memories instead of flashbacks, you'll regain everything that was lost."

"Let's hope so." Pointing across the table to the counter where Raquel kept her tea leaves and other herbs, Dani asked, "What tea concoctions have worked best? Which ones led to days with flashbacks?"

"Well, the one I made you earlier had rosemary and sage. Those seem to work well. And the mushrooms help too."

"Must be why it tasted awful," she said, wrinkling her nose, "but if it works, I'll drink it all day long."

Arianna strode into the room, wiping her hands on a dishcloth. "Dinner's almost ready. And if either of you tell the men I cooked, you're toast." She pointed between her sisters. "I was in the mood for quiche, and the chickens have been giving us eggs in droves, so I made two of them. Raquel's taking credit for cooking though."

"I don't think anyone's going to accuse you of being the 'little woman,' Arianna," Raquel said, making quotation marks with her fingers. "But I love quiche, so your secret is safe with me." She made an X over her heart as her green eyes sparkled under her shoulder-length brown hair.

"Good. Last thing I need is Dominic making fun of me."

"He wouldn't do that," Raquel said, her features contorting with incredulity. "Why are you so hard on him?"

"He's tough and can take it," Arianna said, shrugging. "What's the big deal?"

"Tell me more about Dominic," Dani said, curious about the man who'd lost his sister to the terrible disease that had claimed their mother. "He seems really nice."

"He is to *you*," Arianna mumbled.

"Ari…" Raquel scolded.

"What? It's true."

"He's nice to *all* of us," Raquel said. Reaching over, she covered Dani's hand. "There's a bit of common knowledge you're missing. Dominic is…well, he's kind of in love with you, Dani. It's just something we all accept and don't really acknowledge out loud."

"Ohhhh," Dani said, softly expelling the word as she digested the information. "And he and Maverick are best friends?"

"Yes," Raquel said, squeezing her hand. "Maverick understands you two bonded over Mom and his sister, and he's hella cool about it."

"Wow, that's…weird." Extending her bottom lip, she blew out a breath, fanning the hair at her forehead as she contemplated. "How did two men fall in love with me? What the hell was I doing at the Sendaxa lab?"

"You've always been amazing, Dani," Raquel said, admiration and a hint of longing in her tone. "The prettiest and the smartest of all of us." She gestured between them.

"Speak for yourself," Arianna said, crossing her arms and tapping her boot as her eyes narrowed. "I'm hot in my own fucking way, and most men are pussies who can't handle it."

Laughing, Raquel nodded. "You've always been the most confident and kick-ass, Ari. That leaves me." Her eyes lowered over her body, clad in faded pants and an oversized, baggy shirt. "Chunky and plain. I'm a competent botanist, but I was never chosen by an Ivy League school to run my own lab. Dani's the genius."

"Hey," Dani said, standing and resting her hands on Raquel's shoulders. "I don't want to hear you talk like that, okay? You're my little sister, and you're the most special person on the fucking planet. I'll beat the hell out of anyone who disagrees."

"Thanks," Raquel said softly before pulling out of Dani's grasp. "You've always been my champion. You both have. I was so happy to get recruited by Sendaxa right after they reached out to you. It was the highlight of my career." Her lips formed a sad smile. "Then, the Medical Director told me they'd reached out because you asked them to, Dani. That you wouldn't come on board unless they hired me too. It was above and beyond and I was really thankful."

"I wish I could remember," Dani said, lowering back to the stool and rubbing her head. "But of course I would've wanted you on my team, Raquel. I need your brain. You're smart as hell."

"Thanks." Glancing down, Raquel twined her hands at her waist, and Dani thought she saw her chin quiver ever so slightly. "Well, anyway," she said, lifting her chin. "Enough Debbie Downer for today. I'm going to go feed the chickens before the guys get home."

"I'll help you," Arianna offered.

"It's fine," she said, edging toward the doorway. "I think I just need a few minutes alone. Can't wait for the quiche." Quick as a scuttling mouse, she pivoted and left the room.

"Still the same Raquel," Dani said, sighing as she rubbed the back of her neck. "She just never grew into herself or gained the self-confidence someone as amazing as she should have."

"There's still time," Arianna said, lifting a shoulder. "She's thirty-two, and I grew into myself a lot in my thirties."

"I guess so." Gnawing her lip, Dani asked, "How long did EverLife increase lifespan again?"

"The promise was it would help someone to live to be two hundred years old on average." Arianna grimaced. "Too fucking old if you ask me. Who wants to live that long? Kind of defeats the purpose of having goals, accomplishing them and then using your remaining years to enjoy them."

Dani smiled and leaned her chin on her fist. "What goals do you want to accomplish? All I remember is that you wanted to open your own security firm after you left the military."

"I did, before the world ended," she said with a nod. "Now, I just want to save the world, have a baby or two, and relax somewhere where no one can find me."

Dani's eyes widened with excitement. "You want to have a baby? Aw, Ari, that's so sweet. Aunt Dani is ready to spoil her rotten."

"Okay, calm down," she said, rolling her eyes and holding up her hands. "We've got a lot of shit to do first."

"But once we're done, you'll find a super-hot guy, make him fall madly in love with you and have lots of nieces and nephews for Aunt Dani," she said, holding up a finger.

"A man isn't required in this scenario," Arianna muttered. "Just me, a turkey baster and a nice cabin somewhere in some very dense woods."

The sentiment was quite sad to Dani, who'd always been a sucker for romance and true love. "But you deserve someone who loves you—"

"I've got you and Raquel, and that's enough, believe me." She flashed a grin to soften the harshly spoken words. "On that note, you and Maverick seem good today. I feel for the poor guy. Some days you won't let him near you. Since you're vibing with him today, maybe let him kiss you after dinner."

"He's so fucking hot, Ari," she almost whispered, running her hand through her hair. "It's so bizarre."

"Like Raquel said, you're the catch here. He fell for you as hard as you fell for him. It's kind of sweet. I actually enjoyed your wedding, and I hate weddings." Frowning, she shrugged. "Until Dominic asked me to dance. Motherfucker stepped on my toes a hundred times. That was the first weekend I met him, and I've hated him ever since."

"You're joking, right? Because if you don't want him here, he has to go."

Something flashed across Arianna's face before she scrubbed it with her hand. "He's fine. I'm just being my usual acerbic self. He's actually not a bad fighter. He *might* come in handy one day."

Chuckling, Dani nodded. "Okay, but let me know if you want me to boot him. My loyalty is to my sisters. I'm so glad we stuck together after the world ended."

"No doubt."

"How did that happen anyway?"

Arianna gazed at the ceiling as she recalled the night Dani was injured. "Maverick called me and said they were going on the run with you. Raquel was with them and they wanted me to come. I didn't even think twice."

Grateful for her, Dani felt her features soften. "Thank you, Ari. I'm sure they were thrilled to have someone with your military experience on board."

"Yep," she confirmed with a nod. "I'd been working odd jobs after resigning from the army. But once the world began collapsing, I wasn't working at all. I spent a few weeks wondering if I should go on the run or try to get accepted into a fortified city to perform private security and then Mav called." Lifting a shoulder, she said, "No contest. I was going to protect my sisters. I threw everything I thought I needed into a backpack and met up with you all outside Bethesda. We traveled around a while until we found the farmhouse."

"And here we are," Dani said with awe. "Ready to try and fix everything."

"We'll try our best." Perking her ears, she turned her head toward the doorway. "Mav and Dominic are back. I'm going to go see if they need help. If I'm not back in ten minutes, take the quiches out of the oven."

"Yes, boss," Dani said, saluting.

Once she was alone again, Dani studied the Latin phrases once more before turning to the next page in the notebook. It was labeled "Flashbacks" at the top and had a small list underneath:

*Walking inside the lab and hearing a door creak behind me

*Dominic shaking me as I lay on the floor, screaming my name as I floated in darkness and my head throbbed

*Maverick clinking his champagne glass to mine

Maverick's warmth behind me as his body bracketed mine and his lips brushed my ear

The soles of my sneakers squishing the hallway floor as I retreated from a conversation with someone whose name and face I can't remember. All I could feel in the flashback was anger...uncontrolled rage directed at the person I'd had the conversation with...

Had that conversation been with Luthor Cromwell? Had she tried to tell him they had to stop production of EverLife but he insisted on selling it anyway? Studying the words, she tried to recall the recorded flashbacks in the present moment. Minutes later, she gave up the futile effort. Grabbing the nearby pen, she added a new entry:

Unlatching the door to a biomedical unit and realizing someone was behind me before pain exploded in every part of my skull

"Yikes," Dani murmured, wishing she could recall who'd hit her. The person who'd erased her memory must have worked in the lab. If it was a secure lab owned by a huge biotech company, it was the only logical explanation as to why they would be allowed inside.

Someone who worked with me at the lab had tried to kill me. The thought was extremely unsettling and a vivid example there were very few people she could trust. Whoever they were, they must've been very loyal to Sendaxa if they were willing to kill for them.

It was a mystery that needed solving, and she added it to the mental checklist of things she needed to accomplish.

"Regain memory, steal antidote, reproduce antidote, heal everyone addicted," she said, lifting a finger as she named each task, "*and* figure out who tried to kill you, thus generating your amnesia." Pursing her lips, she almost laughed at the absurdity of the situation. "How in the hell did you get here, Dani? Good grief."

Since the quiet room held no answers, she closed the notebook and headed to the kitchen to focus on the menial task of ensuring their dinner didn't burn. That, at least, was something she could control.

Chapter 12

During dinner, the mood was somber as Maverick and Dominic relayed their encounter with Tristan Holder to the Lawson sisters. Arianna was furious, pounding her fist on the table and exhibiting frustration she hadn't been there to help them. The men reassured her that someone had to stay and protect Dani and Raquel, which was of utmost importance.

"Well, I've never heard of Tristan Holder," Arianna said, squinting at the ceiling as she tried to recall the information. "But he seems like a slimy bastard."

"He didn't kill us, so I'll take that as a good sign," Dominic said. "He certainly is no fan of Cromwell even though he works for him."

"A man who plays both sides of the fence," Raquel said. "Sneaky."

"I can't discern his motives, but he knows ours," Maverick said, sitting back in the chair and running his hand through his hair. "We've got to speed up the timeline, especially since Cromwell knows we're here." Reaching over, he slid his hand over Dani's. "Today's been a long day, so let's have a group meeting in the morning when we're fresh. I'll bring you up to speed early so we can get to work."

Nodding, Dani did her best to process the information, added to the pile of unbelievable facts she'd learned throughout the day. After dinner, Raquel excused herself and headed upstairs to her room. Arianna and Dominic retired to their rooms shortly thereafter.

Once the dishes were washed and the house was quiet, Maverick asked Dani to sit with him in the living room. She slid beside him on the couch, curiosity coursing through her veins.

"Can I...?" She cleared her throat. "How did you fall in love with me? I'm dying to know."

White teeth flashed as he scooted closer and brushed her hair off her shoulder. "I'm not sure I can pinpoint a specific time, but it was probably when I caught you talking to the mice."

She bit her lip to contain her smile. "Occupational hazard. I always got attached to those little critters."

Chuckling, he nodded. "When you first started, I would stand in the hallway outside the lab. But your voice would always carry, and you'd soothe the mice before you injected them with whatever concoction you were testing."

Dani smiled, silently urging him to continue.

"Eventually, I moved inside the lab, content to guard you from inside so I could hear your conversations. You were cute and formidable at the same time. I'd never met anyone as smart as you. You would scribble formulas and run all these equations on your laptop. I was entranced. A genius who cared about mice. It was refreshing."

"Surely you dated."

"I dated," he said with a grin. "And I told myself I'd eventually settle down. My parents had a happy marriage, and I wanted that too. But I wasn't in a rush."

"And you took one look at this and it was over?" she teased, pointing at her face.

His lips twitched, and Dani realized she was thoroughly enjoying the conversation.

"It was a combination of talking to the mice, your intelligence and those pretty eyes. They all hooked me. But I also noticed your determination. You were an unstoppable force, determined to create EverLife so you could move on to your cancer vaccine. You had unwavering purpose."

Dani noted the admiration in his eyes as her body thrummed. They studied each other, smiles curving their lips as she settled into being in his presence.

Maverick yawned before lifting his hand to rub his neck, and she felt the pressing urge to comfort him. It should've been strange, wanting to comfort this man she didn't know. And perhaps there was a slight discomfort in her gut, but it was drowned out by the suddenly voracious need to soothe him after the long day.

"Can we, uh…go to my room?" she asked, her voice raspy. "You look exhausted, and it seems like you've got knots in your shoulders. I can…" Lowering her gaze, she swallowed thickly. "I can try and get them out if you want?"

His lips curved into a slow, sexy grin. "You offering to give me a massage, slugger?"

"Yeah," she whispered, pressing her teeth into her lower lip. "Is it weird? God, this whole thing is so weird. I'm just really grateful for you…and the rest of the team. You've all protected me for months without asking anything in return…*after* I destroyed the world." Tears welled as she struggled to tamp down the emotion burning in her chest. "I just wanted to try and help you for once."

"Okay," he murmured, extending his hand. "Come on."

Sliding her palm over his calloused one, she smiled shyly when he interlaced their fingers and tugged her toward the large downstairs bedroom. They entered, and Dani let go of his hand, crossing the room to switch on the bedside lamp. The door latch clicked, and she realized he'd locked it.

"I'm protecting us from sleepwalkers," he teased when she turned to gaze into his eyes. "I can unlock it if you want—"

"No, it's fine." Glancing at the bed, she crossed her arms over her chest, palming her throat as she wondered what the hell she was doing. Had she really offered to massage him? Now that she was alone with him in a room with a rather large bed, it seemed daunting.

"Dani," he said, the low tone of his voice sending shivers over her skin as he approached. Cupping her upper arms, he soothed her as his hands slid over her suddenly heated skin. "We don't have to do anything. If you want to go to sleep, that's fine. I can give you some solitude. You've had a long day."

Feeling her throat bob, she shook her head. "You deserve a moment to relax too. I guess you should...uh, take off your shirt. Then you can lie down on your stomach and I'll massage your back and shoulders."

Anticipation flared in those gorgeous eyes as he smiled down at her. His height was sexy, and she was suddenly aware of how much bigger he was. Although she was pretty tall, she was lanky and didn't have a ton of muscle definition since she'd worked in a lab most of her life.

Her husband, on the other hand, was chiseled. Bands of muscle ran down his biceps to his forearms, and his torso was thick and firm. Licking her lips, she wondered if the hair on his chest was sprinkled with silver all the way down to his navel. Suddenly dying to find out, she banked the urge to snake her hand under his shirt and trace her fingers over his abdomen.

"Are you sure, Dani?"

"Yes."

He gripped the base of his shirt, dragging it off in one fell swoop before dropping it to the floor. Black and gray hairs swirled over his copper nipples and toned pecs before forming a V that led over his stomach to the waistband of his pants. Touching the tip of her tongue to the dry roof of her mouth, she pointed to his boots. "Take those off too."

He complied, sitting on the bed before removing his shoes and socks. He'd removed his weapons when he returned home, but the belt remained, so he touched the buckle and gazed up at her. "This will be uncomfortable to lie on."

Nodding, she said, "Take it off too."

Thick fingers unclasped the buckle, the movements deft and measured. After sliding it out of the loops of his black pants, he dropped it on the floor and pointed. "Should I lie down?"

Dani nodded, unwilling to speak since she was pretty sure she'd lost the ability to perform basic functions once she'd seen his chiseled chest. He lowered to the bed, sprawling on his stomach and lifting his hands to fluff the pillow a few times. Once it was full, he rested his cheek on the pillow, facing her as he rested his arms at his side. "Do your worst, Dr. Ward."

Dr. Ward. That would be her name if she were married to him, wouldn't it? Wrinkling her nose, she said, "I'm pretty sure I kept Lawson. Mom was a feminist, but she loved my dad and loved that name."

Chuckling, he nodded against the pillow. "Dr. Lawson-Ward. That's what you decided on. It has a nice ring to it."

Grinning, she tilted her head. "It does."

Willing her frozen muscles to move, she rested one knee on the bed, extending her hand to lightly press her fingertips against his back. Maverick sucked in a breath, and she stilled. "You okay?"

He squeezed his eyelids so tight, she thought they might fuse together. Slowly exhaling, his fingers gripped the comforter at each side. "It just feels good to have you touch me, babe."

Unable to control her grin, she willed herself to relax—tough since her heart was two seconds away from violently pounding out of her chest. Situating her other knee on the bed, she slid over him, straddling his thighs as she settled against his body.

"I'm really going to need the story of how you talked me into letting you call me 'babe,'" she said, pressing her palms to his back before digging the heels of her hands into the tight muscle. A deep, guttural groan escaped his throat as she began kneading the firm skin, sending a rush of heat to her core. Could he feel it through their clothes? Turned on by the thought, she continued as he slowly relaxed beneath her.

"We'd been dating a few weeks," he mumbled, eyes closed as his face pressed into the pillow. "You were so cute when you stayed late working at the lab. It was pretty much every night since you were a workaholic, and I remember you waving at me through the glass as I returned from getting a soda in the cafeteria. You had a cheeky grin, and I knew you were going to tell me we needed to cancel dinner so you could work for several more hours."

Breathing a laugh, she said, "Yep. That sounds like me."

"Mmm hmm," was his smooth reply as he emitted another soft moan. The fact he found her strokes pleasurable awoke something inside her. Something that felt a lot like desire and unsated lust. Holy shit, she wanted him. Dani was suddenly very aware she was yearning for her husband as vehemently as a Henry Cavill superfan watching *The Witcher* bathtub scene. Wiping her slightly damp brow with her wrist, she remained silent so he would continue.

"I entered the lab—which you told me not to do because it distracted you. But I entered anyway and came up behind you to tease you for cancelling our date. You swatted me away, but I took the opportunity to sneak in a kiss since you were going to diss me in favor of genetic engineering. I mean, that can really shake a man's ego."

Dani recalled the flashback she'd found in the journal. Was this the moment she'd remembered when Maverick had bracketed her body?

"I leaned down and kissed your neck before whispering in your ear, 'You're going to give me a complex, babe. I finally got you to agree to date me, even though you swore your work was too important and you didn't have time.' You leaned back against me and gazed up at me with those pretty eyes and said, 'Don't call me babe.'"

Chuckling, she said, "I'm with you so far."

"And I pulled you closer and said, 'What if I make you beg for it? Hmmm? Will you let me then?'"

Shivering, Dani attempted to breathe as her throat threatened to close.

"I do love a challenge."

His warm chuckle vibrated through his chest, surrounding her in its warmth as he nodded. "You sure do. Much later that night, I drove you home and you invited me in. You taunted me that I couldn't make you beg." Opening one eye, his lips curved as he stared at her with a lazy gaze. "Let's just say you lost."

Desire hummed as her body threatened to overheat atop his strong thighs. "I...uh...wow. I guess I shouldn't have underestimated your...*abilities.*"

Sliding his hand up her thigh, he gently squeezed. "My ability to love you is my greatest accomplishment."

Tears stung her eyes as emotion overwhelmed her. Frustration she couldn't share in the memories he so obviously cherished. Anger that years had been ripped away from her with one striking blow. Fear at the feelings welling in her chest for a man she couldn't remember but somehow knew.

"Sweetheart," he whispered, his face a mask of concern as he slowly rolled beneath her to lie on his back. "Come here. Lie on your side that isn't hurt. Come on." She settled into his side, allowing him to slide her leg over his thighs. Once they were twined together, he lifted his fingers to her temple and brushed away a curl. "It's okay. Just feel me, honey."

His angular features began to blur as wetness clouded her eyes.

"*Shhh...*" he soothed, kissing her forehead. "I know it's scary—"

"It's infuriating!" she gritted, angrily swiping away a tear. "How dare the universe allow me to marry someone as caring and sexy as you and not even remember it? I guess that's what I get for hurting so many people." A sob escaped her throat. "I've killed so many...and I don't remember anything." Closing her eyes, the magnitude of it all washed over her. "Oh god..."

He whispered her name, cupping her head as she pressed her face into his neck. Huge sobs racked her body as she released all the emotion and anger that had built over the day. She'd awoken to a video of herself explaining the state of the world and her tragic role in it, met her husband she didn't remember, and discovered cryptic notes she'd left for herself along the way. For an instant, she wondered if they'd all be better off if they left her behind and continued the mission alone. Arianna was a formidable, cunning soldier, and Raquel was a brilliant scientist. Perhaps their chances were better without her?

"Don't do this, sweetheart," Maverick said, almost crushing her as he held her, attempting to comfort her as she threatened to drown under the weight of her actions. "It sucks, but we can't change the past. We need you to change the future though." Bringing both hands to cup her cheeks, he lifted her face to his as their heads shared the same pillow. "We need you, Dani. Don't give up."

Sniffling, she shook her head. "I have to save everyone who's left. It's the only way I can go on."

"You will, sweetheart. We will. Or we'll die trying."

Her eyes darted between his as she contemplated. "Have I ever mentioned having flashbacks?"

Nodding, he wiped her cheek with his thumb. "You write them in your notebook along with all the weird Latin phrases no one understands."

Uttering a laugh, she bit her lip. "Yeah, I think they're some sort of breadcrumbs I'm leaving myself, but they don't really make sense."

"Did you have a flashback today?" His tone was soothing as his fingers continued to caress her cheek.

"Yes. I think it was of the instant before I was knocked unconscious and lost my memory."

His eyes widened as he digested the information. "Did you recognize anyone? Any familiar smells or senses that could help us identify the person who attacked you?"

Shaking her head on the pillow, she sighed. "It was like my brain shifted into rewind for a few seconds and then it was gone." She snapped her fingers.

Maverick chewed his inner lip as he pondered. "You've been getting the flashbacks more frequently," he finally said. "I think it's a good sign your memory is slowly coming back."

Dani contemplated for a while before she lifted her head to look at the nightstand. "I want to make another video."

"Okay." Turning, he picked up the phone and unlocked the screen before handing it to her. "Go for it."

She settled back against him, noticing how well her body fit with his as she held the phone high with one arm. Ensuring both their faces were on the screen, she hit record.

"Hi, Dani. I know you're probably still in shock, but it's been a long day, as I imagine all of them are." Glancing at Maverick, she smiled before looking back at the phone. "You're smart enough to understand you have to cut the explanation time each day. The first video is good because it contains a lot of information. But I'm making this second video to tell you to stop having everyone explain things to you for hours after you wake up."

"Dani—"

"No, I need to say this," she said, shushing him. "Dani, the fate of the world is quite literally in your hands, and you've got to put on your big girl pants and go out and fix what you fucked up. You can't do that if Maverick has to spend hours bringing you up to speed and making you feel comfortable each day."

"I don't mind, even if you're a pain in the ass," he teased, chucking her on the nose.

"As you can see, he thinks he's funny, and he's going to call you 'babe,' which he swears you approved somewhere along the way. You're not going to like that, but secretly, deep down, your insides kind of melt when he says it."

"Damn straight," Maverick muttered.

"Shhh!" she scolded before staring back at the screen. "Get to work, Dani. Trust Maverick, Dominic and your sisters. Time is running out and you're practical. You know you can't waste it. Also, there's a hidden message in the Latin phrases in your notebook. Figure it out. Good luck."

Clicking stop, she turned her head on the pillow and grinned at Maverick. "Well, what do you think? Can you make sure I watch that one each morning after watching the first one?"

His eyes roved over her face, filled with admiration and desire, before he took the phone and set it on the nightstand. Rolling over, he slid his hand over her lower back, drawing her into his body as their legs twined below.

"Babe, all I can think right now is that I want to kiss you."

Swallowing the huge lump in her throat, she placed her hand on his jaw. "Tell me about the first time we kissed."

His fingers drew lazy circles on her lower back above her shirt as he spoke. "You were celebrating another failure and roped me into having a sip of champagne with you. It was against protocol for me to drink while on duty, but I'd done it with you a few times before and I couldn't resist..."

Dani was mesmerized by his smooth voice as he recounted the memory...

Maverick clinked his glass with Dani's, overcome by her bright smile and the scent of her hair, even though it was cinched atop her head in a messy bun. He liked her curls down, but there was something adorable when she gathered all that hair and tied it together, baring the line of her neck and the silken skin there. Taken by the sight, he didn't realize he was staring until she called his name.

"Huh?" he asked, lifting his eyes to hers. Setting down the glass, he told himself to back away. "Sorry, I have to get back to work."

"Oh, you're no fun," she said, wrinkling her nose. "And honestly, my workaholic ass isn't much fun either, so I guess we're both a bunch of losers."

Maverick knew he should walk away, but for some reason, he wanted to reassure her. That she was definitely fun. And gorgeous. And brilliant. And somehow, he'd begun thinking of her all the damn time. He'd been head of security at the lab for a few years, but during Dani's tenure, he'd picked up every extra shift available in order to be near her. To see her smile when she arrived each morning and experience her tired wave when she exited after midnight each evening.

To see the way she treated Dominic, whose gruff exterior was no match for her open heart and desire to comfort him due to the loss of his family. Or the way she was with Raquel, who she'd bent over backward for to secure a job at Sendaxa. Maverick understood this because he'd done the background checks on all the applicants, and several scientists were more qualified. But Dani wanted Raquel, so she ultimately got Raquel.

To see how relentless she was in pursuit of the perfect formula for EverLife. It was only a stepping stone on her path to creating a cancer vaccine, and she was determined to finish the project and move on so she could tackle what she considered her life's purpose.

Unable to stop himself, he reached for her, observing his hand as it slid through the air in slow motion. Cupping her chin, he tilted her face to his. "You're not a loser. You're a force of nature, Dani. It's so beautiful. You're beautiful."

Those plump pink lips parted as her eyes widened, the honeyed flecks so pretty under the staid fluorescent lighting of the lab. The vein at her neck fluttered, and Maverick felt himself falling. Never had he been so consumed by a woman. He was a confident man who dated sporadically and never had to search far to find a willing participant to sate any sexual desires. But looking at her...touching her...was different, and he slowly understood why people referred to it as "falling..."

"What the hell is happening?" she whispered, her knuckles white as her fingers tightened on the glass. "Maverick?"

"Set down the glass, Dani," he commanded softly.

Her tongue darted out to bathe her lips, leaving them shiny as his muscles hardened with desire.

"Why?"

"Because I want you to put your arms around my neck when I kiss you."

"I...oh...uh, well, this isn't really...I mean...we can't do that here—"

Grasping the glass, he all but ripped it from her hands and set it on the metal table. Gliding his arm around her waist, he drew her into his warm body. "Slide your arms around my neck."

"I'm a dorky scientist," she rasped, her arms lifting even as she tried to talk herself out of kissing him. "I'm sure there are many other women who'd...fit you better."

"I'm sure there are," he murmured, lowering his head and nudging her nose with his. "But right now, all I can think *about is you." He brushed his lips over hers, gentle and slow, and his knees turned to jelly as she trembled in his arms. "Scratch that. No one has ever fit like you, Dani." Resting his forehead against hers, he whispered, "Ever."*

"Maverick—"

Inhaling his own name from her lips, he devoured her with one relentless stroke of his tongue.

"Wow," Dani breathed, her chest visibly rising and falling as he recounted the story. "That's pretty romantic."

"Sure is." The backs of his fingers skated over her cheek as they stared into each other's eyes. "From that night forward, it was only you, Dani. Forget falling. I dove over the cliff and never wanted to look back."

She ran her tongue over her bottom lip, wishing it was *his* tongue as she shimmied further into his body. A soft growl exited his throat as he pressed his hips against hers, and her heart slammed when she felt his erection against her thigh.

"Fuck," he rasped, closing his eyes as he pulled her close. "I want you so much."

"I want you too," she admitted, acknowledging the pulsing arousal skating through every inch of her body. Her nipples had pebbled into hard, aching peaks, and wet arousal pulsed between her thighs. Heat flushed every cell in her skin, setting it on fire as she slid her fingers through his thick hair and squeezed. "Kiss me, Maverick."

Groaning, he dove for her, clenching her hair and tilting her face to his. His lips pressed against hers, consuming them before plunging his tongue in her mouth and sweeping to taste every crevice. Dani wriggled into his body, desperate to sate the lust that threatened to burn her alive. She tentatively touched her tongue to his, and he rewarded her with a desire-laden groan before urging her to her back and sliding atop her quivering body. He was careful to rest his weight on her uninjured side, and pushed her legs open to press his hard shaft between them.

Dani moaned, overwhelmed with the weight of his strong body against hers. Clenching her hair, he broke the kiss, panting wildly as he undulated his hips into hers.

"Do you feel that, baby?" he asked, grinding his cock into her as her body jutted up to meet his ragged thrusts. "Feel how much I want you?"

"Yes," she groaned, her head lolling on the pillow as her hair skated across the pillowcase. "Oh god, this is insane. I want you too. *Maverick...*"

Pressing his lips to hers, he drew her into another molten kiss, the movements of his hips steady and strong between her legs. Dani's nails dug into his back, causing him to buck against her, and she felt her inhibitions melt away. Twelve hours ago, she didn't even know this man. Now, she was seconds away from ripping away their clothes and begging him to fuck her.

Reaching for her shirt, she began to bunch the fabric to slide it off and gasped. She'd also inadvertently grabbed the bandage, and the resulting twinge of pain shot through her side.

Tensing, Maverick froze and broke the kiss. "Is it your side?" Lowering his hand, he gently grasped her wrist. "Let me look at it."

Sliding off her trembling body, he sat beside her and lifted her shirt. Frowning, he shook his head. "The bandage came off. Let me get another one, and I'll clean the wound."

"I cleaned it when I showered earlier," she said, feeling like someone had thrown a bucket of ice water over her head. Sexual frustration buzzed in her frayed nerve endings as he warily studied her. "I think I should actually leave the bandage off and let it get some air tonight."

Exhaling, he nodded as his warm breath trailed across her skin. "Okay." Gazing at her, he placed his fingers over her collarbone and began to rub the soft skin, soothing her as she relaxed on the bed. "Well, that was fun...for a while at least. Right?" He gave her a goofy grin as a question simmered in his eyes. "It wasn't too much, was it? I never want to cross a line with you, Dani."

"It wasn't too much," she said, disappointed the sexy encounter was over. "Do we...um, how often do we...go all the way?"

Breathing a laugh, he continued to caress her. "Every so often. It's just hard because I don't want to take advantage of you. Earning your trust every day is very important to me, and if I don't have it, I won't touch you."

She slowly shook her head on the pillow. "Thank you."

Smiling, he caressed her cheek one last time before rising. Leaning over, he kissed her forehead and brushed the tiny tendrils of hair away. "I'm going to let you get some rest. We've got a big day tomorrow with a new video. I'm interested to see if we can cut the time it takes for you to settle in and accept your new reality each day."

Placing one last reverent peck on her lips, he rose. "Sweet dreams." Striding to the door, he opened it and turned to face her. "I love you so much, Dani. I have to say it right before I leave because I don't want you to feel pressure to say it back. But it's true, and I hope you'll lock that somewhere in your memory so you can cherish it in your dreams." He gently rapped his fist on his forehead, imitating stimulating the brain to remember. "Night."

The door clicked behind him, the sound almost tangible in the quiet room. As her body attempted to cool from unrealized sexual desire, she rose to inspect her wound one last time. Then, she prepped for bed in the adjoining bathroom, noting her flushed skin in the reflection.

Lowering between the sheets, she glanced at the phone and spoke softly. "Don't let them down, Dani. Listen to yourself on the videos. Time to kick it into high gear."

Clicking off the lamp, she stared at the ceiling, willing herself to be strong enough to quickly accept her new reality so she could fix what she'd so badly broken.

Chapter 13

Tristan strode into the opulent penthouse offices, frustration oozing out of every pore at the senseless loss of life in the earlier confrontation with Maverick and Dominic. His men should've heeded his order not to fire, and it cost them their lives. Now, he'd have to ask Luthor for more men, and he hated asking Luthor for *anything*.

Luthor still kept his offices at the Sendaxa corporate headquarters in DC. Moving into the White House would've afforded too much nostalgia and symbolism to a government that was long gone and would never exist again. He understood he had to build a new society from the headquarters of the company that now controlled the world.

And Luthor Cromwell was the dictator.

After walking through the empty sitting room, Tristan placed his palms on the large wooden doors and pushed them open. Freezing, he observed the display before him as fury ignited in his gut. It swirled and twisted, making him queasy, and he cleared his throat to indicate his presence.

"Oh, Tristan, hello," Luthor said, his gravel-laden, weathered voice making Tristan's skin crawl. His face had aged better than his voice, making him appear middle-aged although he was almost seventy. Running a hand over the woman's hair who was kneeling before him, he chucked her chin. "Thank you, Jessica. You can button your blouse now."

Jessica stood, buttoning her blouse as Luthor stuffed his flaccid cock back in his pants before sliding up the zipper.

Tucking in his shirt, he gestured toward the counter on the far side of the room. "There's a vial of EverLife and an antidote vial to manage the aftermath. Goodbye, dear." Leaning down, he kissed her forehead, and Tristan resisted the urge to march over and kill him on the spot.

It was the least the bastard deserved for the way he treated his sister. She was hooked on EverLife, as most of society now was, and Luthor held that addiction over her head like a fucking twisted pied piper. He had several women in his rotation, and the dance was the same with all of them: they traded sexual favors for EverLife with no end in sight.

The cycle made Tristan want to retch.

He would certainly find the situation terrible if his sister wasn't one of those women, but the fact she'd literally just finished sucking the bastard's dick to fuel her addiction ripped him in half.

And that was why Tristan Holder was determined to murder Luthor Cromwell.

Of course, it couldn't be *now*, since there were two armed guards in each corner of the room. Two men who'd watched his sister suck off a crazed old man who held limitless power. Running a hand over his face, Tristan shifted his weight before placing his fists on his hips. "Go on, Jess," he said, giving her the permission he felt she was waiting for. "I need to speak to Luthor alone."

She nodded, scuttling over to grab both vials before heading toward him. Staring up at him with dull, addiction-ridden eyes the color of his own, she stood on her toes and kissed his cheek. "Thank you."

With a curt not, he dismissed her, furious she hadn't been strong enough not to take the drug in the first damn place. She'd had a messy divorce two years before EverLife hit the market, and the promise of looking young forever was too tempting to resist. She'd been addicted from the first pill, and now she was shooting the shit straight into her veins. It was appalling to Tristan, who'd never touched a drug in his life and never would.

"Did you give her the pure antidote?" Tristan asked, already knowing the answer.

"You know I only offer the pure antidote to people in my inner circle, Tristan," Luthor said, striding over to look over the city he now controlled. The sun was setting in the distance, and he latched his hands behind his back as he stood firm, without remorse, as most monsters did. "The common antidote will ease your sister's symptoms and cravings for a while, which should bring you solace. When they return, she knows where to find me."

The "common antidote" was the name given to the watered-down version of the antidote Dani had created. It was now manufactured in one of the biotech facilities Luthor had seized when he overtook the District. He'd relocated all remaining scientists and manufacturers to the facilities, which now only produced EverLife and the common antidote. Tristan had a feeling Luthor knew about the employees who sold portions to the black-market drug dealers for them to dispense outside the walls. The more people addicted to EverLife, the better in Luther Cromwell's view. It made him indispensable and allowed him to remain the most powerful man on the planet.

"I only agreed to work for you if she's protected—"

"And she is," Luthor interrupted, holding up a hand. "I'm very busy, Tristan. Are you here to update me on Danica Lawson?"

"Yes." Stepping forward, he addressed Luthor as he slid into the leather chair behind his mahogany desk. "I made contact with Maverick and Dominic and confirmed they plan on breaking into the lab even if Dani doesn't regain her memory."

"Good," he said, steepling his fingers and touching them to his lips. "Capturing her crimes on video and televising her trial—and subsequent execution—will cement my place as leader. The people are starting to yearn for a scapegoat, and we can't have them blaming me." He cocked an arrogant brow.

"Wouldn't it be easier to just kill her?"

"No." Lowering his gaze, he touched his palm to the desk and stroked the wood as he recounted his master plan. "The people want a villain, and Dani created EverLife. Her death will be meaningless unless I exploit it for all to see."

"And she'll play right into your hands," Tristan said, flattening his lips.

"Of course. She'll break into the lab to steal the antidote, and my cameras will capture everything. We'll portray her as a thief who wanted to steal EverLife and sell it to black-market dealers."

"And you'll get your scapegoat," Tristan said, crossing his arms over his thick chest.

"I'll disseminate the footage of her break-in and capture to every remaining news outlet. Then I'll put her on trial for the world to see." He flashed a malevolent grin. "With a judge of my choosing, of course."

Tristan had to refrain himself from rolling his eyes at the man's arrogance and haughtiness.

"Once she's found guilty, we'll inject her with EverLife on live TV over several weeks. Get her hooked, throw her into a cell, and let the world watch her die from the addiction."

Rubbing his chin, he asked, "Do you think you could be underestimating the desire people have to watch an innocent woman die?"

"*Pfft,*" he scoffed, slicing a hand through the air. "She's no more innocent than I. She created the drug that destroyed the world."

"She formulated the drug, but *you* funded EverLife and allowed it to be dispensed after you learned of the side effects. You are the villain, Luthor."

The evil man's lips twitched in a humorless laugh. "I've been called the villain for so long it's lost its luster. The fucking government pushed me into this position, with their constant investigations and indictments against me."

"Your company was a monopoly they wanted disbanded. No company should have that much control over a nation's pharmaceutical supply."

"And what did it gain them?" Luthor asked, lifting his hands. "Their persecution of me only made me detest the government more. I began to understand that I was the one who needed to seize control. That people like me would never be safe from their constant oppression."

"Billionaires are rarely oppressed," Tristan muttered. "You had everything you could possibly desire."

"No," Luthor said, frowning. "I had money, but I didn't have power. EverLife was the key I needed to seize control. The system is fair again. Balanced. Those who live in the walls are grateful and play their roles. This is how society should function. The old government was obsessed with tearing down the rich, when all we wanted was the ability to enjoy the spoils of our hard work." Fixing his gaze on Tristan, his eyes narrowed. "We just wanted to be left the hell alone."

"Criminals are often prosecuted by government. That's the way it works, Luthor."

Rising, he jabbed an angry finger as he spoke. "I'd watch your tone, young man. I agreed to let you work for me because you have military skills and I like your sister. I *really* liked having her mouth around my cock a few minutes ago."

Tristan clenched his fists so hard he thought they might crumble and turn to dust.

"But she's expendable and so are you, so I'd suggest showing me the respect I deserve. Now, I'll say thank you for completing your task today and ask you to leave me the fuck alone so I can get back to running the world." He dismissively waved his hand, shooing Tristan from the room.

Pivoting, Tristan stomped toward the door, rage surging at the old man's arrogance. Before he could pull the handle, the door flew open and he closed his eyes. The scent of spring and heartache surrounded him, and Tristan cursed the organ that pounded in his chest.

Lifting his lids, he forced himself not to sneer at the woman who breezed into the room. His expression remained void of emotion as he spoke. "Grace," he said with a slight tilt of his head.

Those ice-blue eyes he saw in every fucking dream widened slightly before her face dropped into an expressionless mask as well. God, they were both experts at hiding the intense emotion that roared within.

Roared within *his* gut, at least. Grace Cromwell hadn't shown emotion in years. Especially not toward him.

"Tristan," she said, that honey-gravel voice almost causing his knees to buckle.

"Ah, my darling wife," Luthor said, striding over and placing a peck on her cheek.

Tristan saw the minuscule flash of distain before she pasted on a smile and greeted her husband. Or perhaps he imagined it. Deep in his mind, a small part of him still hoped his wife hated her husband.

Rather his *ex*-wife. After all these years, he could barely bring himself to say it. His wife now belonged to the man he detested. Dark and sticky anger surged in his veins, and he clenched his fists to ground himself.

"To what do I owe the honor?"

Grace's eyelids fluttered as her fake smile deepened. "I invited the Luddingtons to dinner tonight. George feels left out since you didn't invite him on your lake excursion last week. We need to keep him happy."

Luthor rubbed a hand over his face. "I hate that fat bastard, but he has connections to many of the wealthy in the District who support me. Well done. I'll be on my best behavior."

With a nod, she turned and glanced at Tristan. Her eyes skated over his neck, and flashes of having her soft lips trail over the skin blazed through his brain.

"Tristan," she said, the word husky as she reclaimed his gaze. And then, she was gone. Lost to him as she'd always been.

"How uncomfortable it must be for you," Luthor murmured, "knowing I'm married to your ex-wife and fuck your sister. You have an unbearable tolerance for pain, my friend."

Tristan recoiled and backed toward the door before he gave into his base instincts and strangled the bastard. He needed to protect Jessica at all costs, and attacking the man who kept her alive—for now—wouldn't help his cause. Once

Danica retrieved the antidote, he wouldn't need the bastard anymore. But for now, he needed to retain close proximity to the man he planned to kill one day.

Clenching his jaw, he turned and stalked from the office, anticipating the day Luthor Cromwell expelled his last breath.

Chapter 14

Maverick stood at the stove the next morning, cooking as he anxiously awaited Dani's arrival in the kitchen. He relished the idea of her accepting her current reality without a ton of explanation each day because it would afford more time for them to plan. She usually entered the kitchen wary, and sometimes holding a makeshift weapon like a candlestick or even a shoe, but perhaps the second video would make her feel more comfortable.

Something rustled behind him, and Maverick turned to see his wife standing in the doorway. Inquisitive green irises roved over his frame as he let her look her fill. Finally, she opened her mouth to speak.

"So, um, apparently we have some work to do." She traced the floor with her bare toe as she gazed down. "I'm terrified and have a million questions, but my brain also accepts you're not going to hurt me." Lifting her gaze, she said resolutely, "Bring me up to speed and let's get to it."

Love for her swelled in his chest as he admired her grit and strength. It was one of the many reasons he'd fallen so hard for her, and he couldn't control the desire to touch her. Setting down the spatula, he slowly trailed toward her, opening his arms when he was close. She pursed her lips, contemplating, before she stepped forward into his embrace.

"Good morning, sweetheart," he whispered, kissing her hair.

Drawing back, her fingers clenched his shoulder. "Hi." She gently ran her fingertips over his chest, covered by his black t-shirt. Maverick let her explore, determined to make her feel comfortable.

"Sit at the table and I'll answer anything you like," he said, gesturing toward it before he resumed cooking.

Dani asked him questions as he maneuvered around the kitchen. Eventually, her sisters and Dominic arrived, all sitting at the table and "meeting" Dani as they did each morning. Her resolve seemed firm, and Maverick felt they were crossing a new threshold. It was time to make a solid plan to break into the lab and retrieve the antidote.

After breakfast, they moved to the living room, where they spent hours going over the map of the lab Maverick and Dominic had drawn on a piece of cardboard they'd found in the basement. Eventually, they formulated a plan—one that didn't involve Dani regaining her memory.

"So, we'll just assume Dani will still have amnesia when we attack," Maverick said, pointing at the spot on the map that signified the entrance to the biomedical storage room where she'd hidden the antidote. "You'll still need to scan your fingerprint, Dani, and Dom and I will search the farmhouse basement to find materials we can use to make explosives to hopefully blow open the locks."

"I'm still going to try like hell to remember the code," Dani said.

"I know you will," Maverick said, reaching over and squeezing her knee.

"I have a new tea I created yesterday. It's got some herbs and mushrooms that should help with memory."

"Thanks," Dani said, grinning. "You're my botany whiz, so I look forward to trying it."

"You're both geniuses," Arianna confirmed. "But the rest of us can still kick some ass. Dom, remember that fertilizer we saw in the shed? We could probably use that to make explosives."

"We can combine it with the fuel we collected yesterday and make some heavy-duty IEDs," he said with a nod.

"Great," Maverick said, tapping the cardboard. "Why don't you two work on making those? You can use the empty milk crates and jars in the basement. I'd like to take a quick walk with Dani to make sure I answer any lingering questions. Although the explanation time seems to have been cut shorter by the making of the second video. Great idea, babe."

"Ew," she said, wrinkling her nose.

Emitting a hearty laugh, he lifted a shoulder. "Sorry. Old habits die hard. After we walk, I'll come help you all while Dani works in the lab with Raquel."

"Where do I keep the notes I mentioned in the video?"

"In a notebook we found in the small office off the kitchen." Raquel pointed toward the doorway. "Your notes don't make a ton of sense, but you've always loved being cryptic."

"At least that hasn't changed," Dani said, chuckling as she ran a hand through her hair.

"Okay, I think we've got it," Arianna said, rising. "And I want to spar and do some target practice with you two so I'm prepared when we infiltrate the lab." She pointed between Maverick and Dominic. "Are we set on the timeline?"

"A week is enough time to prepare, I think," Maverick said. "If we're assuming Dani's not going to recover her memory, I don't see any point in waiting longer than that. We've been here for three months, and we need to take action. Our encounter with Tristan proved that."

"Tristian said he didn't wish to harm us, but we don't know if he can be trusted," Maverick continued. "As we prepare, we'll also get supplies ready so we can camp along the way to the first black-market compound after we retrieve the antidote. We'll need to travel on foot once the gas runs out in the truck, and it will be too dangerous to return here."

"Let's hope we get a friendly reception at the compounds," Arianna said. "It's possible they'll be skeptical of our intentions. There's not a lot of trust floating around these days."

"We don't have a lot of options, so we'll do our best," Maverick said. "Having a compound of addicts isn't a fulfilling goal as a leader. Hopefully, the compound leaders want to return to some semblance of normal. If so, we'll begin to recruit militia at the compounds as we cure people. Once we're formidable enough, we'll formulate a plan to take down Cromwell."

"And the Ten Cities will fall too," Arianna said.

"Yes," Maverick nodded. "DC, New York, Miami, LA and all the others that were walled off. I think if we capture Cromwell and liberate DC, the rest will follow."

"And who will lead then?" Arianna asked. "In this new society? You?"

"Uh, no thanks," Maverick said, rubbing the back of his neck. "My only desire is to help Dani save the world and regain her memory." Glancing at his wife, he grinned. "And maybe have a few kids while we're still young enough, but that's a discussion for another time."

"I always wanted kids," Dani said wistfully, leaning back against the couch. "Once I created my cancer vaccine, I was going to have a gaggle of babies."

"Well, let's start with one and see where that takes us," Maverick teased.

Dani contemplated him before her lips curved ever so slightly. "We'll see. I'm still not sure we're actually married. I'm going to need some details."

"Come on, then. Let me debrief you so we can get to work."

Dani stood, ending the meeting as she followed her husband outside under the blue sky.

Chapter 15

D ani's sneakers crunched the gravel as she walked beside Maverick. Biting her lip, she stared up at him. "I need details. How the hell did this happen? How bad is the damage—"

"I try not to focus on the damage with you. It detracts from our purpose."

Stopping short, she faced him, lifting her chin in defiance. "I need to know, Maverick."

Gray eyes roved over her face. "Mav is fine. And I think we should sit for this."

He led her to a large stump, left behind from a nearby tree that had snapped in half. They lowered onto the withered wood as Maverick inhaled a deep breath.

"Sendaxa recruited you five years ago. The CEO, Luthor Cromwell, wanted you, and was prepared to offer anything to get you."

"He offered to fund my cancer vaccine," she said, tracing her fingers over the stump. "Smart play."

"It helped to overcome your objections, and you began working for him. This was a few months before the US government appointed a special council to look into his business dealings." His lips drew into a thin line. "He wasn't a good man. Not only did he falsify clinical trial data of drugs created before EverLife, but he eventually falsified the data from EverLife trials too."

"I must've been livid when I found out," Dani said, exasperated. "There's no way I would've continued working for him."

"You were in a bind. You knew the drug was more addictive than the clinical trials reported—thanks to Luthor's meddling—but you also knew you had the best chance of creating an antidote in the Sendaxa lab. It was state of the art. Nothing else came close."

Her lips fluttered as she expelled a breath. "So, I created a ruse and continued to work there so I could fix what I'd broken."

Maverick nodded. "The FDA fast-tracked the drug, and it began selling over the counter while you worked on the antidote. You were tireless. Dom and I made sure one of us was always there to protect you."

"Luthor believed I was still on board?"

"He had suspicions, but you were convincing. There were times when he visited you in the lab and your discussions became...heated. You eventually cooled off enough to remember your goal. Luthor was rapidly gaining power as more people consumed EverLife, and you had to keep him on your good side to maintain access to the lab."

"Why would he let me create an antidote? If what he wanted was ultimate power?"

"You can't have power if everyone is dead," Maverick said, lifting a sardonic brow. "He needed the antidote so he could water it down and keep people alive but addicted. Addicts are controllable."

Steeling herself, she asked, "How deadly is EverLife? And why the hell did everyone start taking it?"

"Social media is a powerful force. People have been swayed to take drugs for years. You remember the craze surrounding the diabetic drug that also fostered weight loss. Tons of non-diabetics began taking it solely to lose weight."

"But it wasn't addictive," she said solemnly, running her toe over the grass.

"No. For EverLife, you realized you needed to include minute amounts of narcotics in the formula to dilute the pain from the increased cellular manipulation." He flashed a grin. "Making people stay young forever is hard on the body."

"Did I use poppy plant extract? Why in the hell didn't I use Psilocybin or THC?"

"You tried, but they weren't strong enough. The poppy plants were the only pain suppressant that worked effectively...as long as the drug was taken properly."

"The amount a person would have to take in order to become addicted would be extreme. Taking that many pills would rip open someone's stomach."

"You compensated for this in the clinical trials. You had two groups of people take double and triple doses and documented the side effects. One was the destruction of stomach lining, and the other was addiction. People who took the triple doses experienced addiction and needed to go through withdrawal."

"I would've recommended it be categorized as a Schedule II drug so it could be regulated and only available by prescription after consulting with a physician."

"And having a Schedule II drug wouldn't make nearly enough money for Luthor," Maverick confirmed. "He falsified your data, and it was approved by the FDA as a Schedule IV drug, similar to several over-the-counter sleep medicines. Anyone could get it."

"Bastard," Dani breathed, punching the log. "And I was stuck because I needed to stay on his good side to create the antidote in my fancy lab. Geezus. I really dug a fucking hole."

"It got worse when social media got a hold of it. Several reality stars with big followings touted EverLife as the 'miracle drug.' Luthor paid them to promote the drug on their platforms. People began stockpiling the drug and selling it on the black market."

"Which means they didn't stick to the recommended doses."

Shaking his head, Maverick sighed. "Addiction grew in every portion of the country. No race, class or town was immune. People began crushing the pills and injecting them intravenously to experience the high. It was a vicious cycle."

"So many lives destroyed," she said, swiping away a tear. "All because I didn't foresee the inevitable."

"You couldn't have foreseen this, sweetheart," he said, gently rubbing her arm. "You have an optimistic heart when it comes to science. Honestly, I don't think anyone could've foreseen this."

Dani remained quiet, allowing the shocking details of her destruction to settle deep in her bones.

"Luthor became the most powerful man in the world. The president of Sendaxa's board overdosed on EverLife, leaving Luthor in power of the company's massive funds when he dissolved the board shortly thereafter. Without any votes needed to make decisions, he began closing off large cities, urging the wealthy to remain inside where they could obtain EverLife and the watered-down antidote he created from your formula."

"The army didn't stop him?"

"President Johnson overdosed, and Luthor took control of the army, Dani. He ultimately achieved his goal of taking down the government."

"Jesus," she breathed, raking a hand through her hair. "And once he had the antidote, he didn't need me."

"We knew the writing was on the wall," Maverick said, covering her thigh and squeezing. "Dom and I thought he might kill you once he had everything he needed. You hid a secret stash of antidote, and we bided our time so that you could resign and bring the antidote with you."

"And then some fucker hit me in the head," she exclaimed, rubbing the base of her scalp. "I guess we didn't anticipate everything."

"Unfortunately not. We went on the run and scouted safe places to stay. By the time you got amnesia, the world was in chaos. Many houses were abandoned because people had moved inside the Ten Cities or to a black-market compound. We finally found this place, and now it's time to enact our plan. I'd hoped you would regain your memory, but we can't wait anymore. I'm sorry, slugger."

"I get it," Dani said, straightening her spine. "And I can't live with myself until I try to fix this mess." Rising, she faced him and formed a lopsided grin. "You know we're probably going to fail, right?"

Standing, he cupped her shoulders. "Where's my optimistic scientist?" he teased. "I never would've imagined you could destroy the world, but you did."

Dani shot him a droll look.

"So, who's to say you can't save it as well?"

Straightening her shoulders, Dani inhaled a breath. "Good point. Maybe we have a tiny shot." She squinted and held her thumb and forefinger an inch apart.

Laughing, Maverick rested his forehead against hers. "With you at the helm, I like our chances. Come on. We've got work to do."

Dani leaned into her husband's side when he slid his arm around her waist. She sure as hell hadn't meant to decimate the world but knew it was damn well time to save it.

Chapter 16

After her walk with Maverick, Dani entered Raquel's makeshift lab and got to work. As Raquel toiled with combining the various herbs she'd collected over the past few days, Dani read over the notes she'd left in the notebook. She'd warned herself in the video that she was leaving breadcrumbs, and she was determined to decipher the cryptic phrases.

Raquel returned from the kitchen, carrying a mug with steam rising from the center. Handing it to Dani, she said, "This is a brand new concoction. I'm hoping it will help your memory. Drink up."

Dani took the mug, blowing on the hot liquid before she drank. Touching the rim to her lips, she took a sip before breaking into a coughing fit.

"Dani?" Raquel asked, rubbing her back.

"I don't care if that gives me the memory of a fucking elephant," she sputtered, wiping her mouth. "It tastes awful. I'm not drinking it."

Raquel's face fell. "Okay. I was just trying to help."

"I know," Dani said, cupping her shoulder, "and I appreciate it, but I just can't. I'd rather forget my name than drink that."

Something flashed in her sister's eyes—so quick Dani couldn't read it—before it disappeared. Sighing, Raquel nodded. "Okay. Maybe I can try putting some mint in the next one. Sorry."

"It's fine. Thanks for trying."

Raquel circled the table, returning to the other side as she began to fiddle with the various plants and herbs on the table. Dani picked up the pen and wrote in the notebook. *Raquel's teas taste terrible. Stopped drinking them on...* Glancing up, she asked, "What's today's date?"

Raquel informed her it was July 28, and the year was several past the one Dani last remembered, but she jotted down the date anyway, vowing to have a written reminder she hated the teas. It might hurt Raquel's feelings, but there was no use in ingesting something she was pretty sure would make her puke.

Eventually, the sun began its descent behind the rolling hills that met the horizon outside the farmhouse window. Dominic entered, asking them both how they were faring and informing them Maverick and Arianna were still doing target practice. Dominic approached and sat in the open seat beside Dani as Raquel excused herself to get some fresh air before the sun set.

"So, tell me about you," Dani said, observing his scar, which he'd explained at breakfast he'd received during his tour in Pakistan. "Maverick told me on our walk we're good friends."

"We were," he said with a nod, circling his thumbs as they sat atop his thighs. "And maybe we'll be again one day, if you ever get that noggin' to remember." He tapped his temple.

Chuckling softly, she shrugged. "I want that more than you, believe me."

His resulting smile caused tiny wrinkles to form under his eyes, making Dani guess he was somewhere around forty. Weathered enough to have seen combat so fierce he sustained scars but still young enough the wrinkles softened when his lips flattened again. "You were the last person to see your mom alive, and I was the last person to see my sister alive. We both held their hands as they passed from cancer. It's a terrible experience."

"So true," Dani said, blowing out a breath as she shook her head. "Mom asked to see Arianna first, and they said their goodbyes, then I went in next. I probably took too long with her, but I just didn't want to say goodbye." Tears clouded her eyes as she struggled with the emotion blocking her windpipe. "Suddenly, her face fell and she let out this long breath. I called for Raquel, and she ran inside but it was too late. She didn't even get to say goodbye. Mom just slipped away...and I felt so helpless."

"There was nothing you could do," he said, gently rubbing her upper arm.

"I know, but it burns." Rubbing her chest, she felt the fire of failure simmer deep within. "I want so badly to save other people from that experience. Now my cancer vaccine seems so far away. All because I made terrible choices."

"I would argue you made the choices you thought would bring you to a vaccine faster. You couldn't have known what would unfold with EverLife. You're pretty brilliant, Dani, but you're not psychic."

"I guess." Sighing, her teeth toyed with her lip as she pondered. "But one day, I'm going to do it, Dominic. Save people like us from having to suffer."

"I have no doubt."

Gazing tenderly at the kind man who had such a gruff exterior, Dani asked softly, "Tell me about your sister. I'd love to know her story."

Feeling the tension ease slightly from her muscles, she settled in and listened to her friend tell the sweet story of how much he loved his little sister.

Arianna stepped through the back door, loving the slight pain in her muscles after her sparring session and target practice with Maverick and Dominic. She'd been an officer in the army before she resigned, and missed the thrill of always being alert and combat ready. She'd been deployed to Afghanistan twice before receiving another promotion—and realizing that being a female officer in the army was never going to make her truly happy.

The ranks were rife with sexism and misogyny, and although strides had been made, Arianna understood she could only advance so far in a structure designed for men, by men. Her stoic exterior certainly didn't help, but she'd refused to paste on a smile and fake it. Men had told women to "smile more" since the dawn of civilized society, and Arianna wasn't interested in playing that game. Take her or leave her, she was true to herself and there was honor in that.

So, she'd resigned from the army around the time Sendaxa released EverLife to the masses. Dani had been thrilled the FDA fast-tracked the drug's approval since it brought her closer to working on a cancer vaccine. Arianna had been extremely proud of her little sister, who they'd all believed was going to save the world.

Frowning, Arianna smoothed her hand over her half-bald head, wishing they hadn't been so horribly wrong. In the months that followed EverLife's release, addiction spread across the globe, signaling the beginning of society's downfall. And then she'd received the voicemail from Maverick.

"Arianna, it's Mav. Dani's sustained a terrible head injury, and we've been banned from the lab. We've also been placed on the black list for entry into the District. We're going on the run and we need you. Call me when you get this. Everything is going up in flames, and I don't know how long the cell phone towers will be functional."

Arianna had eventually connected with Maverick and joined them as they searched for a place to hide. Thankfully, they'd found the farmhouse, and it had given them a few months of refuge. Now, the time had come to attempt to right Dani's wrongs. Although not intentional, her sister had fucked up royally, and Arianna was determined to help her set things right.

Cynthia Lawson would expect nothing less from her daughters than to help each other through crisis.

Arianna had loved Cynthia with a ferocity she couldn't quantify. She'd been young and most likely unprepared for a child when she adopted Arianna. But they'd learned together—grown together—and Cynthia met Bill Lawson several months after her adoption. He was kind, and Arianna observed him fall like a rock for her adoptive mother. Even though she'd been a child, she understood their connection and thought it beautiful.

They married shortly after Arianna turned five, Cynthia's belly already swollen from the baby growing inside. Cynthia would sing to Arianna, taking her hand and placing it over her stomach as Dani kicked beneath. Arianna had formed a connection with Dani before she was born and relished being the oldest sister. Protecting Dani and Raquel was an honor, and she'd felt a calling to protect them all her life.

Now, she could use the skills she'd learned in the military to help Dani and hopefully save countless others. It was a worthy cause, and Arianna would do her best to achieve it.

After removing her boots and tossing them by the back door, she silently strode toward the den, her ears perking as she overheard Dani and Dominic's conversation. Glancing around the doorframe, she watched them. They shared a comfortable comradery as Dominic spoke about Pam, even though Dani didn't remember their past. Feeling her heart squeeze in her chest, Arianna observed their interaction.

Every so often, Dani would reach over and soothe him, rubbing his corded arm as he recounted stories about his sister. Being nurturing came easily to Dani, and it was one of the reasons Dominic had been drawn to her. Arianna understood this and tamped down the swell of jealousy that threatened to choke her as she listened.

Arianna had always been quiet. Stoic. Thoughtful. And yes, perhaps she was a bit harsh. She was no psychoanalyst but figured it stemmed from the fact she'd always felt the need to prove her worth to her family. Although Cynthia and Bill had adopted her and loved her intensely, the nagging feeling she didn't belong always lingered in the corner of her mind.

She was the adopted sister while Dani and Raquel were blood sisters.

When Arianna was seventeen, Bill was struck by a drunk driver and passed away. It was devastating, and the Lawson family did their best to grieve and move on. During that time, Arianna took on the nagging fear that Cynthia would gain more comfort from Dani and Raquel since they were Bill's biological daughters. That fear caused her to retreat...to sink further into silence so Bill's "real" daughters could grieve with Cynthia.

Cynthia had drawn Arianna back in, pulling her from the abyss of her fears and assuring her she was as much her daughter as Dani and Raquel. But the fear and self-doubt always lingered, even for someone as outwardly confident as Arianna.

Years later, when Cynthia lay in her bed, minutes from death from the cancer that was ravaging her body, she'd called for Arianna. She'd stepped into the dim room, unable to control the tears she rarely shed. Sitting by her mother's bedside, she'd gripped her clammy hand, stroking it as Cynthia struggled to speak.

"You've always been so strong, Ari," she rasped, her green eyes devoid of the sparkle that had lived there for so long. "I need you to watch over the girls. You're the strongest of all of us, and I love you with all my heart."

"I love you too, Mom," she'd whispered, unashamed when a tear fell on her mother's cotton nightgown. "I'll take care of them. I promise."

"Good girl," she said, patting her hand. "You were my first baby and taught me how to love. Don't ever forget that. My beautiful baby..."

She'd drifted off, her eyes drooping, and Arianna had placed a tender kiss on her forehead before rising and allowing Dani to take her place. Cynthia had passed away moments later, before Raquel had a chance to say goodbye. Arianna held her youngest sister, soothing her as she railed at the unfairness of the world and the misery of being denied one last goodbye.

Shortly thereafter, they'd buried their mother and further cemented their bond. The Lawson sisters would always remain loyal and steadfast to each other, no matter the circumstances. It was a promise to their mother they intended to keep, and Arianna was grateful to have Dani and Raquel in a world she found quite lonely.

Gazing at Dani and Dominic, Arianna wondered if things would've been different if Bill and Cynthia had survived. Would she be as harsh and unyielding? When she'd first met Dominic, could she have been the one to offer him a safe place to tell his stories instead of Dani? Could he possibly have chosen to love her instead?

Scoffing, Arianna shook her head, ridding it of the pointless, meandrous thoughts. Long ago, she'd accepted she wasn't meant to have a great love. Some were—Dani and Maverick proved that. But many were also like her. Impenetrable. Different. Outliers. She'd just never understood how to reach out and connect with someone. In the deep corners of her heart, she yearned to offer Dominic comfort. To ease his head against her chest and stroke his short dark hair as he told her about Pam.

In reality, the idea scared her to death. Dominic didn't want someone cold and unyielding to soothe him. Dani was exceedingly better at emotion, and Arianna understood that. Maybe one day, when she had her own child, she could allow herself the space to be vulnerable. To trust she had the emotional bandwidth to truly love and nurture someone...and to be loved in return.

For now, she'd accept the man she loved was better off taking comfort from someone who understood how to offer it completely. Annoyed with herself at the unusually sappy thoughts, Arianna pushed off the door frame and headed upstairs to seek solace in her room before dinner.

Chapter 17

Dani spent the next few days acclimating to her new normal. The wound at her side—which she'd sustained by falling into a pitchfork according to her notes and her sisters—was healing nicely and only stung occasionally. She continued to write more notes for herself, making sure to record instances of small flashbacks and any patterns she could find.

She also began writing notes about Maverick on a fresh page titled "My Husband" at the top. There, she would jot down things she wanted to remember. Every morning, as she watched the video where she intimately cuddled with the handsome stranger and spoke to herself, her heartbeat accelerated furiously in her chest. Armed with the knowledge he wouldn't hurt her, she always rose and headed to find him and her sisters.

The idea she'd fallen in love was so intriguing to Dani, she decided she wanted to write down the little quirks and gestures Maverick exhibited each day. After all, she was a scientist, and the best way to study a subject was to keep copious notes. She hoped to ease herself down a new path where she finally remembered him.

Several days before the planned break-in, she sat at the lab table, reading her list as Raquel toyed with some concoctions across the room. Maverick, Arianna and Dominic were outside training, and they'd fallen into a nice daily rhythm. Dani would wake up, watch the videos and they would all have breakfast. Then, they would sit and study the map as they discussed their plan and theorized ways they could succeed and fail. Maverick would walk with Dani while Arianna and Dominic worked on the IEDs and Raquel toiled in the lab. They would all reconvene for dinner before her sisters and Dominic retired to their rooms and Dani spent some time with Maverick.

Narrowing her eyes, she read the notes she'd left over the past few days.

*Maverick and I had a nice evening. He's funny and has a chip on his shoulder about his parents' love of Top Gun and all things 80s. He's also a great kisser. You tiptoed back into the den to make this note so you wouldn't forget. Make sure you do it again. Soon.

Snickering, Dani closed her eyes for a moment, trying to imagine the kiss. Had his lips been firm against her softer ones? Lifting her lids, she read some of her other missives.

*Maverick knows where your birthmarks are. The one behind your knee, the one on your elbow...and others. It's so weird but also kind of hot. Like he's touched you in places that only belong to him...

*Maverick was so sweet as he tucked you in tonight. He kissed you and then walked to the door and turned around before telling you he loved you. It wasn't timid or shy, like several of the duds you dated in the past. He said it so firmly, with that deep voice that makes your insides vibrate. "I love you so much, Dani." God, it makes my knees shake as I'm writing this. I think you need to trust him enough to go all the way...

And then, there was the note from last night:

*Okay, Dani, enough is enough. You're writing this in the dark as parts you don't think about in polite society are quite literally throbbing. Maverick just kissed you like your lives depended on it and left you sweaty and needy in a lonely bed. You have a dangerous mission ahead of you and might not survive. For god's sake, let him hold you. Let him love you. He's safe. You know that deep within even if your brain can't recall the memories...

Sucking in a breath, Dani lifted her gaze to the ceiling, contemplating. Could she really make love to a man she only remembered meeting that morning? Chewing the top of her pen, she didn't notice Raquel approach until she was right beside her.

"Okay, this one should taste better," she said, her gaze slightly wary as she extended a mug. "If it's too cold, let me know."

Flipping through the notebook, Dani pointed at one of her entries. "Sorry, sis, but I have a written directive not to drink any teas you make. I also made a note to tell you that you're amazing, remind you I love you and not to take it personally."

"Okay," Raquel said, her eyes drifting to the notebook. "Can't mess with the notes," she teased. "It also seems like you're having more flashbacks, which is a good sign."

"Yes." Turning to the page where her flashbacks were recorded, she tapped it. "I'm having at least one flashback every day, sometimes two." Excitement bloomed as Dani felt herself inching closer to regaining her memory. "I feel like we're close, Raquel."

Her sister stayed silent a moment before she smiled. "I hope so. In the meantime, I'm going to take a walk and drink the tea since you don't want it." She took a sip as her eyebrows rose in delight. "This one actually tastes good. See you in a bit."

After Raquel stepped outside, Dani flipped to the page with the Latin phrases. Zeroing in, she felt drawn to them for some reason. Reading in a hushed voice, she recited the words.

- *Fere libenter homines id quod volunt credunt* (Men generally believe what they want to)

- *Nemo mortalium omnibus horis sapit* (Of mortal men, none is wise at all times)

- *De omnibus dubitandum* (Be suspicious of everything)

- *et tu, Brute?*

Frustration consumed her as she tried to decipher any hidden meaning. Sadly, it was no use. Annoyed, she flipped the notebook closed and rubbed her tired eyes.

Pushing away from the table, she decided she needed some fresh air before the group gathered for dinner.

Chapter 18

During dinner, Maverick observed Dani, grateful for her progress over the past few days. Although her memory hadn't returned, she'd had several murky flashbacks, making sure to record them all in her notebook. Her disposition seemed more resolved and also...*lighter* in a way. It reminded him of when they'd met. The focused head of security and the meticulous, steadfast scientist. Each drawn to each other in ways they couldn't explain but somehow made sense.

After dinner, Dani and Maverick headed to the living room, leaving Dominic, Arianna and Raquel to a raucous game of poker at the kitchen table. As their shouts of disbelief at their misfortune and bursts of laughter echoed through the house, Dani snuggled into Maverick's side on the comfortable couch as he gently rubbed her arm.

"Did you have a flashback today?" he asked, loving her resulting shiver as his voice washed over her. She'd told him often how sexy his voice was, and he reveled in how her body still responded to it, even if her mind didn't remember.

Picking at a stray thread on her pants, she nodded. "It wasn't anything tangible though. I keep seeing the lab and the biohazard symbols...but that's all I can remember."

"Hey, it takes time, sweetheart."

She hesitated, biting her lip as she contemplated. Finally, she said softly, "I do have several notes where I tell myself to..." Her cheeks flushed as her gaze tentatively lifted.

Sliding his fingers under her chin, he grinned as he stared into her eyes. "Yes?"

"I told myself to...let you kiss me...and touch me." Her eyelids squeezed together. "Oh god, this is embarrassing."

"I love touching you," he murmured, reveling in the swirls of emotion that clouded her eyes when they popped open. "But I won't push you. We can just sit here and relax if you want. We've only got a few days until the shit hits the fan, and I'm happy to just hold you."

She studied his face and throat, from his angular nose to the muscles that were corded in his neck from her tender caresses. Curiosity entered her expression and she cleared her throat. "How long has it been since we had sex?"

Maverick couldn't resist teasing her, considering she looked so serious, and he relished making fun of her when she fell into a serious mood. "Did you have a flashback about us having sex? That's hot."

Wrinkling her nose, she laughed and swatted his chest. "No. I just...I was just wondering. Forget it."

His deep chuckle blanketed them as he leaned closer, brushing his lips across her ear. "It's been a while, babe. I miss you."

A dull ringing sounded in his ears as breath rushed from her throat. Her chest lifted in a chaotic rhythm as his body hardened. Consumed by her, he waited, determined to let her take control.

"How long?" she whispered, her voice raspy.

His tongue darted out to bathe his parched lips as he slowly drowned in her scent. Letting his eyes rove over her pert nose, dash of freckles and plump pink lips, he stopped trying to control his jagged heartbeat. How could he when she looked at him like this, inquisitive and stunning, with her lithe body pressed against his? Placing his fingers at her temple, he tenderly tucked a curl behind her ear.

"Honestly, it happened more in the beginning...before we ran out of wine and beer." Cocking a brow, he gestured with his head to the kitchen. "Every once in a while, when we first moved here, you would get tipsy at dinner and after that..." He drifted off, shaking his head as he grinned. "I don't want to sound like a creep. I never seduced you when you were drunk or anything. I just—" He rubbed a hand over his face. "You're always more...*open*...when you're tipsy, and if we had a good day, you'd drag me into your room. I made sure to ask several times for your consent. Promise." He made an X over his heart.

Dani expelled a breath, her cheeks puffed as she digested his words. "It's true. I like to get down when I'm tipsy."

Laughing, he tugged a strand of her hair. "One of the many things I love about you. Two glasses and you're a sure thing."

Enchantment at his teasing marred her features, and she bit her lip, almost sending him over the edge as her teeth toyed with the flesh. "But then we ran out of booze?"

"Yeah." His fingers trailed through her tresses, the soft strands silky against his skin as they spoke. "There wasn't a huge stash anyway, and we fell into our roles. We began formulating a plan for when you recovered your memory and hoped like hell it would happen."

"Until dead bodies started disappearing and a stranger appeared to tell you to get on with it."

"Yep," he said, chuckling as he nodded.

She remained silent as he traced his finger over the smooth skin of her jaw. He continued the caress, moving lower, causing her to shiver as he drew tiny circles on the sensitive skin of her neck. Sensing her acquiescence, he tilted her face to his and waited for her to speak.

"Maverick?"

"Hmm?"

"I want..." Inhaling a deep breath, she straightened slightly. "I want to make love to you."

A ragged breath escaped his lungs, washing over her as his eyes narrowed and grew heavy with desire. Continuing to trace her neck, he remained silent.

"I mean...if you want to. I—"

"I want to," he interjected, gently squeezing her neck, the possessive gesture causing her to close her eyes as her body swayed toward his. Maverick knew she loved it when he took control, and her body always arched into his, which drove him wild. "I just want you to be sure, babe."

Lifting her lids, she cemented her gaze to his. "I'm sure. Although, I have no idea how I ever let you call me that—"

His fingers snaked up from her neck, covering her lips as she gasped. Sliding his free hand to her ass, he palmed the flesh and dragged her against him. "Give me ten minutes and I'll show you," he rasped, pressing his forehead to hers.

A small eternity passed for Maverick before she nodded. "Deal."

A growl ripped from his throat before he pulled her into his lap. Sliding an arm under her knees and one under her back, he rose, lifting her in his arms. Exiting the living room, he called to the kitchen, "We're going to bed. The door will be locked. See you all in the morning."

"Woo hoo!" Arianna called from the kitchen. "Mav's getting laid. Nice job!"

"Fucking peanut gallery," Maverick muttered, striding into Dani's room and kicking the door closed.

Her melodious laughter filtered through the room as he placed her on the bed. "Arianna's still so fucking acerbic. I love her."

"I love her too, but she's a ball buster," he said, slowly covering her body with his as he sunk his fingers into the thick tresses that fanned across the comforter. "If I didn't love you so much, I'd tell her to fuck off."

Tossing back her head, she laughed, baring the delectable skin of her throat. Unable to resist, Maverick touched his lips to the soft skin, grateful to taste her once more. Sucking in a breath, she plunged her fingers into his hair, tugging as she pulled him closer.

"Show me," she pleaded, her hips undulating to meet his. "I need to see these 'babe-inducing' skills in action."

Chuckling, he placed tender kisses along her neck, gently running his tongue over the smooth skin before nipping her with his teeth. Her body quaked, and he surged the hard ridge of his erection against her mound, frustrated at the barrier of clothes between them. "I'm going to make you scream, Dani." Lifting his head, he clenched his hands in her hair. "But be honest with me, okay? I can get...carried away." He waggled his eyebrows.

The little vixen just smiled and slowly lifted her arms above her head on the mattress. "I'm all yours and I won't break. Just be careful with my side. It's healing nicely, but let's not take any chances."

Lust racked his frame as he gazed at her beauty, sprawled before him like a feast he was ready to devour. Rising, he gripped the hem of her shirt, heart pounding in anticipation of seeing his wife's pretty little breasts for the first time in so damn long...

Chapter 19

D ani observed her husband as he loomed over her, his broad shoulders blocking the light from the bedside lamp as he fisted her shirt in his broad hands. Bands of muscle flexed in his arms as he tore the shirt from her body, and his expression turned reverent as he placed his fingers atop her collarbone. Slowly dragging them across her flushed skin, his breath was heavy as he toyed with the top of her functional bra.

"I'd tell you to rip it off, but I'm guessing we don't have a ton of extra clothes lying around."

A sultry smile crested his lips as he shook his head. "No. We need to keep this one intact." Sliding his hands beneath her, Dani arched her back so he could unfasten the clasp. Tossing the garment to the floor, Maverick rested on his elbow, gazing at her breasts as he cupped one in his palm.

"I think about these pretty little breasts all the time," he murmured, lowering his head to nudge the underside of her breast with his nose. "And your scent…" Inhaling deeply, he breathed her in. "God, Dani, you smell so good. Once I drank you in, I never wanted to let go."

"I wish I could remember," she warbled as tears stung her eyes.

"We'll remember together, sweetheart," he said, repositioning so he could press his lips to hers. He kissed her softly, massaging her lips with his as he breathed her name. "Kiss me back."

Gliding her arms around his neck, Dani tugged him close, opening her mouth to draw him inside. He groaned, surging his hardness between her thighs. His tongue tasted and explored, and Dani almost giggled at his zeal. It was as if he'd been on the verge of starvation and she was his only source of sustenance.

"And what are you laughing at?" he teased, nipping her nose.

"You're so into it. And I'm *really* into it. Holy shit, we have awesome sex, don't we?"

Laughter bounded from his throat as he tossed back his head. Joy emanated from his strong frame, and Dani's heart splintered at his laughter. It brought her almost as much pleasure as his lips against hers, and his hand against her breast. *Almost.*

"We do," he said, grinning as he placed soft kisses along her wet lips. "Since you're thirty-five now and I'm seven years older than you, we always joked we didn't have time to waste having bad sex. We know what we want and are forthright enough with each other to ask."

"I'm on board with constructive feedback, although I don't remember turning thirty." Furrowing her brow, she touched the corner of her eye. "Do I have wrinkles?"

"I wouldn't care if you had a thousand wrinkles" was his sweet reply as he kissed the place she'd touched. "You'll always be gorgeous to me. You're my wife, hon. I'm kind of stuck with you." He winked as she emitted a soft laugh.

Palming his cheeks, she shook her head against the comforter. "You've been so patient. So loyal. Arianna and Raquel both told me today, and I wrote it in my notebook several times." Running her thumb over his bottom lip, she asked, "Do I deserve this? I mean, I destroyed the world. I should probably be in prison."

"We're going to fix it, slugger. For now, just feel, okay? Can you do that for me?"

She nodded, cupping his cheek as she whispered, "Don't let me kill the vibe. Sex first, then save the world. Got it."

Low-toned laughter vibrated in his chest as his hand caressed her breast. His shaft pushed against her thigh, hard and ready to claim her as she shivered. Widening her legs, a sense of female satisfaction coursed through her when he groaned. Pressing his forehead to hers, he gazed at her with a question in his eyes.

"Keep going," she said, her tone shy as anticipation bloomed deep within.

He pecked the tip of her nose before sliding down her body, his hand reaching to cup her breast once more. Touching his lips to the small mound, he began to trail kisses over the quivering skin. Bringing his other hand to the other breast, his fingers surrounded both nipples as he kissed the valley between them.

"*Ohhhhh...that feels so good...*" she moaned, writhing beneath him.

"You like it when I pinch these tight little nipples and kiss you here," he rasped against her skin. Extending his tongue, he licked her, wetting the flesh between her breasts as his fingers tugged and toyed with the sensitive buds.

Tossing her head back, she closed her eyes and mewled beneath him.

Strong fingers twirled and pulled the tight points, shooting a rush of moisture to her core. Squeezing her eyelids together, she felt the warm honey flow between her thighs, aching to relieve the intense pressure.

"Do we use protection?"

"You have a contraceptive implant." He tapped her arm, indicating the location. "We were going to wait to have kids until you cured cancer."

"Got it. So you're safe and I'm safe, right?"

Resting his chin between her breasts, he gently squeezed one of the soft mounds. "Look at me, sweetheart."

Dani lifted her head, overwhelmed with the emotion...with the *love* shining in his eyes. "You're *always* safe with me. Do you hear me?"

Nodding, she licked her lips, rapt with anticipation as his lips curved. "Good girl." Lowering his head, he blew a warm breath on her nipple, causing her to moan. "Now let me taste you, honey."

Lost in the most erotic moment of her life, Dani watched him open those firm lips before closing them over her nipple. Threading her fingers in his thick hair, she clenched the tresses as he sucked her deep, each corresponding pull of the nub throbbing in her deepest place. Soft moans leapt from her throat as he worked his mouth, wetting the flesh as he lavished her with his tongue.

After thoroughly devouring her nipple, he kissed a wet pathway to her other breast. Touching his tongue to the tip, he flicked it several times, chuckling when she groaned in frustration.

"You're teasing me," she rasped, her lips forming a pout. "Please, Maverick."

Forming a sexy smile, he tilted his head. "Beg me again, babe. Fuck, I like it so much when you beg. That's how I originally gained nickname approval." Waggling his brows, he nipped her sensitive bud.

"*Please*," she cried, unable to deny him since her body was slowly combusting beneath him. "Call me whatever you want. Please just don't stop."

"Never." Cupping her other breast, he gently massaged it as he lowered his mouth over her nipple. Dani squirmed against the maddening ministrations, realizing her husband had already learned how to play her body like a musician performing a beautiful symphony. Giving in to the pleasure, she closed her eyes and let him work her nipple on his tongue. He moaned against the quivering flesh, indicating his mutual desire, and she allowed herself to feel a moment of happiness.

Yes, tomorrow would come and then the day after, and eventually they would try to save humanity. But for now, Dani was content to lie in her husband's arms and experience pleasure instead of sorrow for a small window of time.

Once her nipples were wet, turgid peaks, Maverick moved lower, kissing her stomach and abdomen before dipping his tongue in her navel. Dani shivered and pushed her waistband, longing to be naked so he could go lower. Rising to his knees, he shucked her pants, tossing them to the floor before removing his shirt.

"Take off the rest," she commanded softly, loving the arousal that flared in his eyes.

Standing, he removed his pants and hooked his fingers around the hem of his boxer briefs. "You sure?"

Biting her finger, she nodded from the bed. Giving her another sultry wink, he pulled off his underwear before facing her on the bed. His erection stood firm and full, jutting from the springy hairs between his thighs, and her mouth began to water. Firm, ridged muscles skated across his abdomen before leading down to his pulsing cock and thick thighs. God, he was gorgeous. Thanking the universe for the fortune of finding him, she grinned and hooked her finger.

"Come back here and play with me."

Lowering to his knees, he gripped the back of her thighs, drawing her across the comforter as she squealed. Placing one leg over each of his shoulders, his gaze burned as he stared into her eyes. "I give the orders here, sweetheart."

Gasping, her body arched as he pressed his fingers to her folds, spreading her apart and burying his face in her wet warmth. Speaking became a lost cause, along with thinking and most likely breathing as he swiped his tongue over her silken slit.

"You laughing at me?" he teased, the words murmured into her deepest place.

"I'm laughing because I...*oh god*...I might lose the ability to breathe." Pushing against him, she silently begged for more. "And honestly, I don't care."

Knowing laughter reverberated against her wet folds. Sliding his fingers through her slickness, he dragged them to the tiny nerve-filled nub. Warm breath skated across her tender skin as he began to slowly circle her engorged clit.

Clenching the covers, she shook her head in frustration, needing more pressure. Gripping his hair, she undulated into his fingers, her body on fire as her core brushed his lips. "*More...*"

Her husband took pity on her, increasing the pace of his firm strokes as he touched his tongue to her opening. Whispering words of praise and desire, he sipped her honey, sucking her wet skin into his mouth before pressing his tongue to her dripping core. As his fingers circled and stroked, he impaled her with his tongue, darting it inside before retreating and surging back for more.

The act was so intimate...so *raw*...that tiny flames of arousal consumed her. They blossomed into blazes, threatening to burn her alive as her skin flushed a thousand shades of red. Moaning her husband's name, Dani let him take her to heaven with his skillful tongue and incessant strokes. Stars formed behind her closed eyelids, bursting in the dark, until she opened her mouth in a silent scream. Unable to hold back, she dove over the cliff into a blinding orgasm, her husband purring moans of approval against her swollen flesh as she crashed into the abyss.

Shudders racked her frame, engulfing her as wave after pleasurable wave enveloped every cell of her skin. Feeling her muscles liquify, she collapsed on the bed as Maverick rested his cheek against her inner thigh. Sighing, she lifted her head, biting her lip to hide her smile at his smug, satisfied expression.

"Oh man," she sighed, collapsing back on the bed. "I see how you got me to agree to the endearment. I didn't stand a chance."

Rising, he slinked over her body, firmly planting one knee and then the other on the mattress. Slithering over her, sexy and lithe as a snake stalking his prey, he slowly aligned his body with hers. The spiky hairs that covered his body pressed into her sweaty skin, and Dani ran her calf over his, delighting in his growl of approval.

Resting his elbows at her side, he slid his fingers into her hair, massaging her scalp as his cock searched for her. Gray eyes locked with hers as he began to push inside.

"Dani," he whispered, cementing his lips to hers in a torrid kiss as he pressed inside, inch by slow inch. "I've missed this so much."

"I'm sorry," she whispered, aching to comfort him...hating she'd ever denied him anything.

"No, sweetheart," he whispered against her lips. "No apologies. I just need to feel you." Pushing deep inside her tight heat, his length pulsed against her inner walls. "That's it. Open up for me."

Dani widened her legs, allowing him to press farther, his sensitive tip pressing against the inner spot he seemed to intimately know. His fingers continued their pleasurable assault against her scalp, maneuvering the skin around her damaged brain, almost as if he were trying to heal her.

"I don't need to remember to know this is real," she whispered, digging her nails into his neck. His resulting hiss resonated in her bones as she undulated against him. "Show me, Mav. I just need you to show me."

His strong hips began to move, dragging his steel through her softness. Her body mourned the loss every time he retreated and shuddered each time he filled her once more. Gazing into her with hooded eyes, he whispered unintelligible words she somehow understood. Never had she experienced a connection so intense. Needing him to know, she opened her mouth, frustrated when she could only emit a soft mewl.

"I know," he breathed, the pace of his hips increasing as he hammered into her. "It's always like this..." Brushing his lips against hers, his words ripped her heart open. "I love you so much, Dani."

The intensity of the words choked her, breath halting in her lungs as she struggled to amalgamate her feelings with the lingering notion she'd lost every memory they'd ever made together.

"No thinking," he commanded, sliding one hand down to cup her ass as he continued to increase the pace. "Just concentrate on taking me deep...right there." Circling his hips, his cock stroked her clit before jutting inside and reaching the spot deep within.

"Ohhh...*fuck!*" she cried, closing her eyes as his pounding became swift and furious. Clenching her hair, he anchored her, slamming inside her as another orgasm threatened to take hold.

Searching for a stronghold, she gripped his shoulders, finding the muscles strained and rigid beneath her fingers. A ragged groan leapt from his throat as he closed his eyes.

His cock filled her, sliding through her honey as his jaw clenched. Jabbing her nails in his flesh, Dani succumbed to another climax. It burst through her, dragging her into its depths as Maverick stiffened above her.

With one last thrust, he cried her name before burying his face in her neck. Jerks and spasms overtook his frame as he emptied himself into her. Dani squeezed him tight, feeling him pulse against her inner walls as his release jetted into her body. Eventually, his jerks turned to slight tremors as he settled against her. Wrapping himself around her, he pulled her into every crevice of his body.

Dani settled against him, craving his warmth as her body cooled. His fingers toyed with her hair as his lips nuzzled her neck, and he shivered as she slid her nails up and down his back. They lay there for a small eternity before she felt him begin to slip from her body.

"Damn it," he whispered, sighing against her neck. "I don't want to move."

"Let's get under the covers so you can hold me."

Lifting his head, he gazed at her with wary eyes. A dull throb pounded deep within as she realized he wasn't going to stay. Pecking her lips, he lifted on straight arms and said, "Be right back."

Dani's eyebrows drew together as he rose and walked to the dresser. Opening the drawer, he pulled out a cloth before returning to the side of the bed. Silently, he pushed her legs open and wiped away the evidence of their loving. His eyes bore into hers, resolute, silently informing her he couldn't stay. After cleaning himself, he reached for his underwear and slid them on.

"Maverick?" she asked, feeling her heart crumble into tiny pieces as he frowned.

"It never works if I stay, sweetheart," he said, sitting on the side of the bed and caressing her leg. "You wake up and have no idea who I am and usually want to slug the shit out of me." The corner of his lips twitched. "I mean, it's kind of hot, but it's not conducive to us having a productive day."

Feeling exposed, she tried to cover her body before he lifted her from the bed. Holding her against his warm chest, he pulled back the covers and placed her inside before drawing them up to her chin. Kissing her forehead, he cupped her jaw as she stared up at him.

"You won't even cuddle with me? After all that?"

Sitting beside her, he shook his head as he tried to explain. "The problem with cuddling is that I fall asleep in about three seconds. Your body's just too warm, and I'm used to sleeping against you."

Tugging her lip between her teeth, she processed his words. They made sense logically, but her heart wasn't getting the message. "Can't we try? I can make a video."

A brow arched over those gunmetal gray eyes. "That's a lot of videos to watch when you wake up, sweetheart."

"I'll make one to watch first. Come on." Shooing him off the bed, she lifted the covers, urging him to crawl under. "Leave the underwear on. That's definitely less creepy."

A laugh escaped his lips. "Dani, it's not going to work—"

"In. Bed." She pointed under the covers. "Now. You just banged me senseless, and I want to cuddle, mister."

His features contorted with love and affection as he contemplated. Inhaling a deep breath, he nodded and slid in beside her, taking the side closest to the wall so she could reach the nightstand.

"Okay," she said, picking up the note that said *Watch Me, Dani* and making sure it was visible on the nightstand surface. Shimmying underneath the covers, she threw her leg over Maverick's thighs, pressing against him as she lifted the phone high and pressed record.

"Dani, you're going to be scared shitless and that's okay, but take a look at this man." Glancing at Maverick, she planted a kiss on the tip of his nose before turning back to the phone. "He just gave you two amazing orgasms, and you refused to let him leave. *You* asked *him* to stay. He's very special to you, and I need you to not freak out."

Turning her head on the pillow, she grinned. "Now, tell future Dani you won't hurt her."

"I won't hurt you." The words surrounded her as he stroked her hair, gazing into her eyes instead of looking at the camera. "I love you, Dani."

Glancing back at the screen, she gave a cheeky grin. "Dani, if you mess this up, I'm disowning you. You're safe with Maverick, and you still need to ask him why his parents gave him that ridiculous name."

He rolled his eyes at her teasing.

"Now, go watch the next two videos and they'll explain everything. Be cool, okay? You scored a super-hot dude, and you have *way* more important shit you need to focus on. Capisce? Bye for now." She waved at the screen before saving the video and placing the phone on the nightstand and clicking off the lamp.

Turning into his body, she nuzzled against him, releasing a satisfied sigh when his strong arms surrounded her. Sated and content, she inhaled his musky sandalwood scent until her eyes drifted closed.

Chapter 20

Dani clawed toward consciousness, trying to escape the darkness as her eyelids fluttered. Opening them wide, she gasped, turning her head on the pillow to survey her surroundings. A man lay next to her, his broad back facing her. He appeared to be naked, and her eyes drifted to where the sheet rested against his waist. Why was she in bed with a naked man? Had she gotten drunk and had a one-night stand? It was certainly against her nature, but her sleepy brain couldn't devise any other plausible scenarios.

Looking toward the other side of the room, she noticed a note on the nightstand beside a cell phone. *Watch me, Dani.* Although she desperately wanted to run, her arm reached for the phone, almost as if in slow motion, and lifted it. Tapping the screen, she pulled up the videos. With a nervous glance toward the man softly snoring beside her, she pressed play.

Confusion clouded her brain as she watched herself on the screen. In bed. With flushed cheeks and a bright smile, stating everything would be okay. That she was safe.

The man next to her stirred, slowly rolling over until he pierced her with his deep gaze. Sliding his hands underneath his cheek, he relaxed into the pillow, watching her as she debated starting the next video.

He remained quiet, and she didn't sense any danger. Looking back at the phone, she played the next video.

In all, there were three videos, all of them explaining the events of the past few years, her memory loss and who the man next to her was. Her husband. The man next to her was her *husband*.

Setting the phone on the nightstand, she turned to her side, facing him as blood pounded through her veins. Resting her cheek on the pillow, she stared into his eyes, feeling a palpable connection although she'd never laid eyes on him.

Sliding her legs over the cool sheets, she grimaced. Sympathy marred his expression, and he lifted a shoulder. "Last night was the first time in a while. You're probably sore...down there and on your side. You had an unfortunate incident with a pitchfork."

"Yikes."

His lips twitched. "It's healing nicely and shouldn't hurt too badly anymore."

The deep timbre of his voice soothed her as she studied him. As her mind processed the wealth of information she'd just absorbed, her nostrils flared. Shaking her head on the pillow, she asked softly, "How many people did I hurt?"

"Sweetheart," he said, gingerly moving closer, asking permission with his eyes and open expression.

Dani nodded, and he drew her into his arms. Clutching on for dear life, she buried her face in his neck and let the tears fall.

Minutes later, she told herself to get it together and lifted her head to look at her...husband. Resting her face in her hand as her elbow dug into the mattress, she tenderly touched his nose. Tracing the angular feature, she continued tracing his eyebrows before reaching the skin beneath his eyes, marred with slight wrinkles that were way too sexy. Moving toward his chin, she caressed the stubble there.

"Maverick," she whispered, the name slow on her tongue as she felt it out. "At least your parents didn't name you Goose."

"Every fucking time," he droned, playfully rolling his eyes.

Although she was an emotional wreck, his sentiment was funny and she breathed a laugh. "Is it your real name?"

Full lips curved as he nodded. "It was the movie my parents watched on their first date when they were seventeen. Dad fell for Mom on the spot, and when they left the theater, he took her hand and told her he was smitten."

"Aw. Cute." Dani bit her lip.

"Yeah. Well, Mom wasn't as into him and told him she wasn't feeling it. Dad bet her he could make her fall in love with him. She thought him so ridiculous she almost laughed him off the sidewalk and told him if he accomplished the task of making her fall in love with him, she'd name their first kid Maverick."

"Yikes. Talk about a hell of a bet."

Chuckling, he nodded. "Well, she lost, but in the end, they both won. They had a very happy marriage and had me. I was their only kid or maybe they would've had a 'Goose.' We'll never know."

"Where are they now?" Dani asked, hoping they hadn't been a casualty of the drug she'd created.

"They'd already retired to Florida when shit hit the fan with EverLife. There was a cruise ship senior citizens could buy a lifetime ticket for if they had enough money. Mom and Dad had just enough. I urged them to go, and I imagine they're somewhere safe in the Atlantic Ocean enjoying the last years of their life. I want them as far away from what's left of society as possible."

"And if we save everyone?" she asked, resting her hand at the juncture of his neck and shoulder. "Can I meet them?"

"They love you," he said, chucking her nose. "And yes, if it's ever safe for them to return to land, I'd love for them to meet you again if you haven't regained your memory. Especially if we can set things right *and* have a baby. They'd be amazing grandparents."

"A baby," she whispered, fear squeezing her throat as she tried to accept the fact she'd fallen asleep a single scientist in New York City and woken up a married amnesiac. "How old am I now? Thirty?"

"Plus five years, slugger." His lips formed a tender smile. "But still as beautiful as the day I met you."

Swallowing the lump of emotion, her brain scrambled to accept she'd lost so many years. Anger and frustration swelled before it was overtaken by the rumbling of her stomach.

"I know it's overwhelming, but you need to eat." Smoothing her hair, he smiled, and her insides quivered from the flash of his straight, white teeth. "Arianna and Raquel are here, and you can meet Dominic...again."

"You said we haven't..." Gazing down, she pressed her thighs together. "Do we...uh...do that often?"

"No," he said, shaking his head. "But apparently, you've been making some naughty notes in your journal, Dr. Lawson-Ward. I might have to punish you." Mirth sparkled in his eyes, along with a hefty dose of desire. "I will say, this is the first morning I've woken up beside you and you haven't tried to slug me, so we're definitely making progress."

A tiny laugh escaped her lungs. "You're funny."

"One of the reasons you fell for me," he said, his tone cocky as he arched a brow. "You never had a chance, babe. This face with my sense of humor?" He pointed at himself. "I had you from Day One."

"I'm not sure about that, but I'm open to hearing the story." Pushing up from the mattress, she grinned. "On that note, I'm guessing we have a lot of shit to accomplish."

Rising, he pecked her lips before climbing out of bed. "We definitely do. We're going to break into a highly secure lab and steal a secret antidote in a few days." Extending his hand, he waited. "Can't wait to tell you how we plan to do it."

Placing her hand in his, she rose to start another day and learn everything again for the very first time.

Chapter 21

T he next few days were serious and solemn as the crew prepared for the break-in at the Sendaxa lab. They all knew the plan presented serious challenges, but the time for action had arrived.

The plan was simple. Dominic and Arianna would approach the building first, attacking the Sen Force soldiers who guarded the outside. Then, they would blow open the front doors with the homemade IEDs and continue down the long hallways, taking out guards along the way until they made it to the lab. Maverick and Dani would follow behind, Maverick armed to protect his wife the entire way.

Dani would scan her finger to open the hidden secure biolab compartment, which would lead them to the second door with the unknown ten-digit code. Arianna would keep watch outside as Dominic and Maverick blew open the door and Dani retrieved the antidote. Then, they would high-tail it out of Bethesda and reconvene with Raquel, who would be waiting ten miles away in a hidden wooded area.

After that, they would head to the first black-market compound and make contact with the leader in the hopes he or she was receptive. If so, they would find lodging with a generator, set up a makeshift lab and Dani would replicate the retrieved antidote.

As the team sat in the living room one morning, two days before the break-in, Arianna rubbed her hand over her head as she sighed. "We've gone over it a thousand times now, guys." Standing, she began to pace, flexing her fingers as she paced back and forth. "I can't do it anymore. We've got it. Even Dani's got it," she said, pointing at her sister, "and she can't remember shit."

"Thanks," Dani mumbled, rolling her eyes.

"Well, it's true," Arianna said, slicing her hand through the air. "Dom, let's spar before it rains. I need to kick someone's ass before the sky opens up. See you outside."

Stalking from the room, she disappeared down the hallway before the front door slammed, causing Dani to flinch.

"She's just tense," Dominic said, standing and rubbing the back of his neck. "We all are. Tristan said he might leave weapons in the shed but, so far, nothing. Of course, we have no reason to trust him, but extra weapons would be nice. See you all in a bit."

Once his broad shoulders retreated, Raquel stood, wiping her palms on her pants. "I need some fresh air too. I'll be back in a few."

She flitted from the room, leaving Dani and Maverick alone.

"Everyone is tense as hell," Maverick said, harshly rubbing his forehead. "We need to be aligned if we're going to succeed."

"We're only human," Dani reassured him, rubbing his shoulder as they sat on the couch. "It's normal to feel anxious."

"Yeah." Blowing out a breath, he stood. "Come on. Let's take a break and clear our heads before it rains."

They headed outside, strolling around the house before stopping at the shed behind the kitchen. "This is where Tristan is supposed to leave weapons for us?"

"Yes," Maverick said, lifting the latch. "But so far, we haven't seen—" Breaking off, his eyes widened as he opened the door.

"Maverick?"

"Holy shit," he said, drawing the door back so they could both look inside.

"Whoa," Dani said, taking in the menagerie of rifles and handguns that sat strewn on the dirty wooden floor. "Guess ol' Tristan came through after all."

Eyes filled with disbelief and relief cemented to hers. "Well, I'll be damned. I guess he did."

Straightening her spine, Dani steeled herself. "Do I know how to shoot these?"

"I've done some target practice with you and Raquel, but neither of you are fans of semi-automatic rifles. You're both better with a handgun. Raquel carries one sometimes when she heads out on her own and wants space from Arianna and Dominic."

"Fine. Select a handgun for me and let's go practice. You, Arianna and Dominic are fierce, but I should be armed too."

Hesitating, he lifted his brows. "You sure, slugger? We're trained soldiers and I'm confident we can protect you."

"I'm sure." Extending her hand, she turned her palm up. "Give me a gun and let's practice."

Cocking his head, he said, "All right, then. Fair warning: I get really turned on when you hold a gun."

Tossing back her head, she broke into joyful laughter. "Then we *really* need to practice. Let's do it."

Chapter 22

Tristan stood in the shadows, the forest dim from the tall oaks that offered shelter. He'd come to drop off the weapons and had parked at the other end of the forest so his jeep wasn't spotted. At the edge of the trees, a row of mushrooms grew in the grass where the meadow began. A woman bent down, tugging several of the mushrooms from the ground. Every so often, she would grunt if one was stuck, but eventually, she would remove it and continue on.

Careful to remain silent, he watched her work. Eyeing the mushrooms, he wondered why she was picking that particular variety. Curious, he deliberately stepped on a twig, crunching it with his boot to alert her of his presence.

Whirling around, she dropped the basket and placed her hand over her heart. Wide, light green eyes roved over him as he approached. Reaching into her pocket, she pulled out a gun. Lifting it, her hands violently shook as she aimed it straight at him.

"Don't move a muscle, buddy, or I'll blast a bullet into your heart."

Chuckling, he stepped forward, silently admiring her fortitude. From what he'd heard, Raquel Lawson was the quiet younger sister who lived in Danica's shadow. He hadn't expected her to have grit.

"You've got the safety on," he said, arching a brow. "Can't really blow my brains out unless you fix that."

She emitted a frustrated huff before sticking her tongue between her teeth and fiddling with the safety. Closing the distance between them, he yanked the weapon from her hand and tossed it aside.

"Hey!"

"Calm down, little mouse," he said. "I'm not going to hurt you."

"Well, I might hurt *you*," she said, her eyes darting to the gun. "I can dive for that thing, and I'm closer."

"Let's save the drama," he muttered. "Now, why don't you do me a favor"—he gestured toward the basket—"and tell me why you're picking poisonous mushrooms."

"I don't have to tell you anything." Lowering to pick up the basket, she turned and attempted to walk away. Tristan grabbed her arm, tugging her back and stilling her. Fury flashed in her eyes as she glanced down at the basket.

"Don't try and hit me with it," he said, surprised at the mirth in his tone. "My cause of death can't be 'death by basket.' That's really lame."

"Who are you and why are you following me?" she asked through clenched teeth.

"You answer mine and I'll answer yours. Why are you picking false morels? They're toxic."

"None of your fucking business."

Tristan smirked, unable to believe the frumpy-clothed woman was holding her ground. She was young with an air of innocence that reminded him of Jessica before things turned so horribly wrong. Noting the protective swell, he studied her.

"You can't use those in any foods or formulas..." he murmured, rubbing his chin before recognition dawned. "Unless you want to harm someone."

"Small doses of toxic fungi help with efficacy of formulas and teas," she said, jutting out her chin. "Not that I would expect *you* to know that. It's something only a botanist with years of training could comprehend."

Tristan grunted, doubtful but willing to admit he was no scientist.

"My sister is sparring just over that hill." Her finger jutted toward the horizon, which was rapidly filling with dark clouds. "If I scream, she'll be here in a heartbeat. If she sees you harassing me, she'll kill you."

Nonplussed by her threat, Tristan rocked back on his heels, taking in her appearance as he pondered. She was different than the rich, snooty women he was used to inside the walls of the District. Her innocence hadn't been shattered by their dark world, and he found himself hoping it never would be. He hadn't been able to save Jessica from traversing her torrid path, but he hoped this woman never felt the ravages of addiction or pain.

"*Excuse you*," she droned, waving her hand in front of his face. "I'm going to tell you one more time. Leave me alone—"

"I just dropped a shit-ton of weapons in your shed," he interjected, pointing toward the farmhouse. "So I don't appreciate the tone."

Her expression fell as she studied him. "Thank you. That will help the others with the raid."

Tristan's eyes darted between hers. "You aren't joining them?"

"I'm not a soldier" was her soft reply as she shook her head. "They're going to reconvene with me when they're finished."

"Hmm..." Narrowing his eyes, he asked. "And what will you do if they fail?"

"Failure isn't an option."

Admiration surged at her confidence, even though it was unwarranted. Although he hoped Dani and her team succeeded, the chances were small.

Stepping back, he placed his hands on his hips and regarded her. "If they fail, you're welcome to search me out in the District. You'll need protection if they don't return to claim you."

She scoffed. "Thanks, but I'm all set."

Before he could respond, a gun discharged from the far-off hill, and Tristan could see Arianna Lawson's tall figure as she sprinted toward them.

"Gotta go," he mumbled, turning to jog back into the forest. Looking back over his shoulder, he warned, "Don't die because you're stubborn. Search me out if you need me."

Her muttered "*Like hell*" followed him into the woods as he ran back to his jeep and started the engine. Hightailing it back to the District, his thoughts drifted to Raquel Lawson. She had a conflicting purity and defiance that didn't make sense to his logical brain.

Tristan lived in absolutes. A person was generally good or evil in his world. There was no in between. But for some reason, as he drove on the withered gravel, he couldn't shake the feeling there was more to Raquel Lawson than met the eye.

CHAPTER 23

D ani rushed to meet Raquel and Arianna as they hurried to the back door. Rain fell in large drops, intensifying as her sisters stepped inside. Worried, Dani gripped their shoulders.

"Are you okay? We heard a gunshot."

"Thank you for checking on me," Raquel said, pulling Arianna into a hug. "He snuck up on me and I was terrified." Drawing back, she looked at Dani. "I was picking mushrooms, but I dropped them all when he confronted me. I was going to try putting false morels in a tea tomorrow. They have a slight toxin known to increase memory output. If you'd agree to drink it, which I know you probably won't." She gave a resigned shrug.

"A slight toxin, huh? Should I be worried?" Dani teased.

"I would've tried it first," Raquel said, grinning. "And you know as well as I do that a small amount of toxicity can jumpstart neuron function."

"That's true," Dani said with a nod. "Enough about mushrooms. I'm just glad you're okay." Slipping her arm over Raquel's shoulders, she led her into the living room.

Arianna followed, and they sat on the couch as Dominic and Maverick entered.

"Do we know who the perp was?" Dominic asked.

"I'm assuming it was Tristan Holder," Arianna said. "Six two, black hair, lean but muscular?"

"That's him," Maverick said with a nod. "He must've been returning to his vehicle after dropping off the weapons."

"Well, he scared the crap out of me," Raquel said, expelling a breath as she held her hand over her heart and sank into the couch. "Geez."

"I didn't deem him a threat, especially since he left us the weapons," Maverick said, his brow furrowing. "Did he threaten you?"

"No. He was just an arrogant jerk. If I see him again, I'm going to kick him in the balls."

"Atta girl," Arianna said, rising and patting her sister on the shoulder. "I always knew you had it in you. Come on, guys." She gestured toward Dominic and Maverick. "We need to check on the IEDs in the barn. The rain is harder than I expected, and we're probably going to need to plug some leaks so we don't ruin the explosives before we have a chance to use them."

Maverick stood, cupping Raquel's shoulder and squeezing. "Do you need anything from me?"

Dani's heart quivered at the reverent show of affection from her husband toward her sister.

"I'm fine. Thank you, Mav."

"Sure thing." After placing a tender kiss on Raquel's forehead, he followed Dominic and Arianna through the doorway.

"Whew," Dani said, scooting closer to Raquel and rubbing her arm in soothing strokes. "Close call."

"Yeah. I'm fine now. Sorry I freaked."

"It's okay. That must've been scary as hell. Where were you picking mushrooms?"

"Over by the edge of the forest."

Gnawing her lip, Dani saw the logic of trying something different. "I see why you wanted to try, but I'm done with the teas, Raquel. I've had more flashbacks without them anyway."

"Thank god."

Wetness clouded Dani's eyes as she studied her little sister. "I'm scared to leave you while we raid the lab," she said, the words thick with emotion. "What if something happens to you?"

"I'll be fine," Raquel said, drawing her into a hug. "You're going to steal back the antidote, and I'm going to help you create a kick-ass remedy that will cure everyone. As I told Tristan, failure isn't an option."

"I love you," Dani said, drawing back and chucking her chin. "Mom made me promise to take care of you, and I take that vow very seriously."

"I can take care of myself," Raquel said, smoothing a hand over Dani's hair. "You're the important one in this scenario."

"Don't say that." Dani squeezed her hand. "You're important too, Raquel."

Something flashed across her face—so quickly Dani almost missed it—and then the reverent expression returned before she stood. Wiping her palms on her thighs, she uttered a soft "Thanks. I'm going to take a shower. I just need some time to process the encounter. It was intense."

"Of course. Let me know if you need anything."

Raquel nodded before scampering away. Resting back on the couch, Dani crossed her legs, her foot shaking back and forth as she contemplated. Tensions were high and they all were on edge. Hopefully, they would regain some composure before the raid.

If they didn't, Dani worried they would make mistakes, and mistakes were unacceptable. Fear crept in as the importance of their mission preyed on her weary soul.

Chapter 24

The next afternoon, Arianna clenched her jaw as she fired several rounds into the target. She didn't want to waste them, but it was important her aim was sure for the raid. And, if she was being honest, she was pissed as hell that Tristan Holder had approached her sister without Arianna knowing. It was her duty to protect her sisters, and her failure to uphold that vow churned in her gut as her finger pulled the trigger.

Lowering her gun, she cursed as she realized she was out of bullets. She didn't want to use any more since they needed them for the raid, so she clicked the safety in place before throwing the gun on the ground in a completely pointless, annoyed gesture that alleviated a twinge of her frustration.

"You're supposed to shoot it," Dominic's voice called behind her. "Not throw it."

Whirling around, she almost took pity on him. He'd picked the wrong time to meddle with her, and she was good and ready to attack. Sucking in a breath, she pointed her finger in his face and opened verbal fire.

"You son of a bitch! If you ever sneak up on me again, especially when I have a gun in my hand, I'll stick it in your neck and fire a bullet right into your jugular."

The sun was beginning to set over the horizon, leaving gorgeous streaks of orange and yellow in the cloud-filled sky. His scar seemed to glow in the warm colors as he scowled, and Arianna wondered if he was going to yell back. Usually, when she ripped into him, he responded with acerbic comebacks that shot tiny little thrills down her spine. She loved verbally sparring with him more than physically sparring, and that was saying a *lot* since she wasn't a big fan of talking in general.

"Well?" she asked, extending her hands at her sides as exasperation consumed her. "Are you just going to stand there? No quippy comebacks today?"

Approaching her slowly, as if she were a snake about to strike, he drew close enough she could smell his evergreen scent. His proximity shot all sorts of unwanted rushes to her nether regions, filling her with rage. Flaring her nostrils, she wavered between the urge to scream and the yearning to close her eyes and inhale his musky scent until it invaded every corner of her lungs.

He opened his mouth to speak, hesitating as he worked his jaw. Finally, he said softly, "What happened to Raquel isn't your fault."

"Yeah? Tell that to my dead mother. I promised to protect them. *Both* of them."

"And you do. Brilliantly. But even you aren't perfect, Arianna."

Scoffing, she kicked the ground with her toe. "I never claimed to be perfect."

He blinked several times, as if processing what to say next. His indecision drove her insane considering it went against his nature. One of the things she loved about Dom was his assurance and confidence. Clenching her fists so she didn't do something awful like punch him, she began to stomp off. "I don't have time for this—"

"Ari," he said, encircling her arm. "Wait."

Yanking her arm from his grasp, she picked up the gun lying in the nearby grass and aimed it directly at his face. "I told you never to grab my arm again," she uttered through clenched teeth.

Sighing, he rubbed his hand over his short hair, frustration emanating from his large frame. "You're out of bullets, but you can point it at me all day if it makes you feel better."

"What will make me *feel* better is if we accomplish our mission so I can get on with my damn life. I can reclaim my independence, and Raquel can live with you three weirdos who don't seem to give a shit you're both in love with the same woman."

Anger flashed in his eyes as he studied her. "You know, I always wondered why it bothered you so much. My feelings for Dani." Stepping closer, he balked when she cocked the gun, the gesture symbolic even though it held no bullets. "Jesus, Ari. Why the fuck do you even care? You obviously hate me."

A sob escaped her throat, sending shockwaves of embarrassment through her frame at the small outburst of emotion. Arianna never exhibited uncontrolled emotion, especially near Dominic, who was smart enough to sense her feelings if she slipped and bared herself to him. Craving solace, she tossed the gun to the ground and began to stalk away.

"Ari—"

"Leave me alone!" she yelled, angrily swiping a tear that never should've fallen. Goddamnit. Tears had no place in their world. What the fuck was wrong with her?

Clutching onto the silver lining that tomorrow they would attack the lab and begin the next phase of their lives, she took several calming breaths as she stalked across the nearby field. Stepping into the adjacent woods, she collapsed to the ground and rested her back against one of the thick oak trees as she drew her knees to her chest and began to rock.

Placing her hand over her pounding heart, she cursed her feelings for the millionth time.

"Get it together, Ari," she chided, gently rapping the back of her head against the tree. "You aren't the first person to fall for someone in love with someone else, and you won't be the last. This emotional baggage has got to go. Tomorrow's a big fucking day."

Willing her heartbeat to return to normal, she reminded herself there were more important things at stake than her stupid heart. After the break-in, she could sulk and rail at the world all she wanted. *Alone.* As she damn well preferred.

Rising, she wiped the dirt off her butt, inhaled a deep breath and strode back to the house, determined to keep her feelings buried so deep inside they no longer existed.

After dinner, the mood was heavy as everyone packed and prepared to leave the following morning. Once his meager belongings were stuffed into his backpack, Dominic walked outside to place it in the truck, craving fresh air.

The bed of the truck was filled with the weapons Tristan had supplied and the IEDs he and Arianna had made together. Smirking, Dominic found it fitting he and the stubborn woman had found one thing they could make together without killing each other: bombs. Yep, that sounded about right, considering the way she'd blown up on him earlier.

Dominic had no idea why she detested him so vehemently. He figured it sprang from the protective streak she carried for Dani, but she had to realize by now he would never harm Dani or act on his feelings. They were a shield more than anything and helped him cope in a life where he'd lost every person he loved.

Halting on his trek back to the house, he spotted Arianna in the moonlight. Tall and regal, she stood facing the far-off hills, her eyes closed as she inhaled the warm air. Her half hair was in a braid, cascading over her shoulder to rest against the curve of her breast under her tight black tank top.

Dominic had never seen Arianna in any state of vulnerability. She always carried an air of impenetrable toughness. But now, watching her in the shadows, he stood frozen, mesmerized at finally seeing the woman inside. As the silver light washed over her skin, she appeared...sad. Something cracked in his chest at her forlorn expression, and he realized it was his heart. Placing his palm over the organ, he rubbed, barely able to breathe as he gazed at her.

She slid her fingers to the back of her neck, massaging the tense muscles as she sighed. Blood pounded in his veins as the image of replacing her fingers with his own took shape. What would she do if he trailed toward her, gently pushing her hand away so *he* could comfort her instead?

Had anyone ever comforted Arianna? Frowning, Dominic realized it was doubtful. Arianna was a protector. A warrior who felt it her duty to show strength so others could achieve their dreams and goals. When Maverick had asked her to join their cause, she didn't hesitate.

It was noble and selfless to put others' goals and dreams before her own, but what did that mean for *her*? Didn't she have dreams she wished to fulfill? Strangely, the need to find out roared inside, and Dominic promised himself he would be gentler with her. He'd always been harsh to mirror her tone, which was as far away from puppies and butterflies as humanly possible. But now, observing the slight hunch of her shoulders and the heartbreaking aura of loneliness surrounding her, he realized it was a defense mechanism.

If there was one thing Dominic excelled at, it was defense mechanisms. He'd had his own iron-clad defenses for years.

Inwardly chiding himself for lingering longer than he should have during her moment of solace, Dominic forced his legs to move. Entering the kitchen, he headed to his room, content to enjoy the soft bed. It might be the last time he slept in one for the foreseeable future, and he would relish a good night's sleep.

Usually, as he drifted off, his mind would remain blank, pushing away the day's events so he could reset during slumber and wake up fresh. But tonight, for some inexplicable reason, he fell asleep to the image of Arianna's neck glistening in the moonlight as her fingers massaged the soft flesh.

Chapter 25

M averick rose with Dani as the sun was peeking over the horizon. After watching the videos, she understood that today held great importance. As light streamed through the window, she felt grateful they would have a sunny day for the raid. Although she wasn't superstitious, she decided to take it as a good omen. Perhaps they would prevail and begin to set things right.

After breakfast, they huddled in the living room to go over the plan one last time. Around noon, they placed their bags in the bed of the pickup truck and tidied up the home. Perhaps someone else would find it in their travels and it could offer them safe haven as well. Closing the doors behind them, Maverick slid behind the wheel of the truck as Dani and Raquel sat beside him. Dominic and Arianna sat in the bed of the truck, tasked with keeping an eye on the explosives. They weren't set to ignite without being lit with the lighter Dominic had found in one of the kitchen drawers, but one could never be too safe.

They drove over unkept roads, some gravel and some paved, and Dani noted the eeriness of her surroundings. There were no other cars on the road, no people to pass, and the vastness of the consequences of her actions overwhelmed her. Because of her, people had been pushed into black-market compounds or walled-off cities to seek shelter. Society had been irrevocably altered, and the journey back seemed daunting.

"You okay?" Maverick asked, reaching over and squeezing her hand as they puttered along in the truck.

She nodded and willed the emotion away, understanding it wouldn't solve anything. Only their actions could set things right.

The stumps of downed utility poles dotted the horizon, confirming she'd relegated the world to darkness. They passed a row of houses that had been badly burned. Only a few shards of glass remained in the shattered windows. The front doors were marked with red or black Xs, and she wondered what they meant. Most likely red for houses where bodies remained and black for homes that were merely abandoned.

Who was left to bury the dead? How many had died, addicted and alone?

When they passed a large field, Dani craned her neck, attempting to identify the mass of crumpled metal in the tall grass.

"It's a helicopter," Maverick said. "Or, it was. Probably ran out of gas and crashed. Hopefully the pilot and passengers survived."

"I hope so," Dani said softly, overcome with the devastation. Tears burned her eyes, but she knew they were pointless. Crying wouldn't resolve the situation. Action was her only course.

Twenty miles from Bethesda, they spotted two forms in the distance, lying on the side of the road. Maverick slowed, parking several yards away before exiting and drawing his handgun.

"You two stay here," he said to Dani and Raquel. "Dominic, come with me. Arianna, keep them safe."

Arianna gave a salute from the bed of the truck as Dominic hopped out and pulled his gun. Their broad shoulders grew smaller as they approached the bodies, and Dani lifted her fingers to her lips as she observed Maverick kneel and shake his head. The scientist in her yearned to examine the situation, needing to understand what happened. Disregarding Maverick's orders, she exited the truck and approached.

"Sweetheart," he said, rising and showing her his palms. "You don't want to see this."

"What did they die of?" she asked, inching closer. "Were they addicts?"

"It appears so," Dominic said, his tone sad. "They exhibit the traits of EverLife addiction."

Swallowing thickly, she lifted her chin and urged Maverick to step aside. "I need to see the damage, Maverick. It will only make my resolve stronger."

Deep eyes contemplated before he nodded and backed away. Stepping toward the two bodies, Dani gasped as she took in their disheveled corpses. Dark bags stretched under their eyes, which barely seemed attached to the sockets. The female's mouth was open, showing only one tooth and gums that were rotted and scabbed. The man's lips were chapped and caked with dried blood, and there were infected puncture wounds in the crook of both his elbows.

"They were shooting it intravenously," she murmured, crouching to get closer. "It was destroying them from the inside out."

"The bodies aren't decomposed, so they must've died recently," Dominic said.

"Two lives ended with such senselessness," Dani said, pressing her fist to her mouth so she wouldn't scream.

"Hey," Maverick said, encircling her arm and pulling her to stand. "That's not going to help us here, Dani. Your sadness and guilt are justified, but focusing on it just makes things worse."

Glancing back at the bodies, she expelled a long, slow breath. "You're right. We need to bury them though. It's the least I owe them. To give them a proper resting place."

"We'll bury them," Dominic said, cupping her shoulder. "There's a shovel in the truck bed I decided to bring with us. I wasn't sure we'd need it, but you can never have too many blunt objects." Training his gaze on Maverick, he said, "Let's bury them and then get back on the road. We need to drop Raquel off and get to the lab before sundown."

"I can help," Dani offered.

"Let us do it," Maverick said, rubbing her arm. "Go sit with Arianna. Have her tell you about our wedding. She wasn't a fan of Dom's dancing." Dominic scoffed.

They headed back to the truck, Dani crawling in the truck bed with Arianna as Raquel joined them. Dominic and Maverick buried the bodies as the sisters spoke. As they recounted stories about the weekend wedding that happened years before the world fell apart, Dani studied her sisters. Reaching over, she squeezed both of their hands.

"I love you both so much. Thank you for sticking with me after what happened. I understand if part of you wants to hate me for the destruction I caused."

"We could never hate you," Raquel said. "We're family, and Mom would want us to support each other."

"What she said," Arianna uttered, grinning to soften the harsh tone. "You're stuck with us, Dani."

Maverick and Dominic returned, and after washing their hands with some of the soap and water from their supply stash, the trip resumed. Eventually, they made it to the location ten miles from the lab where Raquel would camp until they returned to retrieve her.

Once she was settled in the clearing in the dense woods, she hugged everyone before nervously twisting her fingers as she spoke. "I'll be sending you all the good vibes, guys. Just think, eight hours from now, you'll be back here with the antidote, and we'll be on our way to making things better. You've got this."

"You remember how to use the gun?" Arianna asked.

"Well enough," Raquel said with a shrug. "It's only a few hours. I'm going to rest in the sleeping bag and try to relax. Don't worry about me. Go kick some ass."

After one last round of hugs, they left their sister behind, ready to enact their plan.

CHAPTER 26

As the last rays of light glimmered over the horizon, the team arrived at an abandoned parking lot two hundred yards from the Sendaxa lab. Exiting the truck, they began preparing, buckling duty belts and arming themselves with guns, knives and the IEDs. Dani was given a handgun, which Maverick assured her he'd trained her to use, while the three soldiers were much more heavily armed.

They snuck through the woods surrounding the lab, Maverick leading as he observed the entrance. "Two soldiers flanking the door and four additional soldiers visible surrounding the building," he whispered.

"Confirmed," Dominic and Arianna said in unison.

"Dominic, you'll take out the soldiers on the right flank, Arianna will target the ones on the left. Shoot to wound first, but if you need to make a kill shot, do it."

They both nodded.

"Remember the plan?" Maverick asked Dani.

"Once they take out the guards, you and I will head inside. I'm to stay directly behind you in case we encounter guards along the way. You'll lead us to the storage area in the lab where I hid the antidote. I'll scan my finger to unlock the first door, and you'll use the IEDs to blow open the second door. Ari and Dom will keep an eye on the outer hallways to protect us."

"Pretty good for a woman whose memory is broken," he said, pecking her lips. "Remember, stay near me at all times. I can't lose you, Dani."

Dani's heart leapt in her throat as she nodded, the magnitude of the mission truly washing over her. They were going to break in to a heavily guarded lab to steal something that was sealed behind nearly impenetrable locks. The chances of success were slim, at best.

"It's this or let the world continue to crumble, Dani," Maverick said, squeezing her wrist. "We have to try. You won't forgive yourself if we don't."

Exhaling a shaky breath, she straightened her shoulders. "I'm ready."

Her husband flashed a grin filled with admiration and resolve before turning and beginning to advance toward the edge of the woods. Lifting his fist, he extended his fingers and began lowering them in a silent countdown. Three. Two. One. Slicing his hand through the air, he gave the soundless order for Arianna and Dominic to advance.

They crept toward the edge of the trees, Arianna aiming her rifle at the guard on the left side of the door, Dominic aiming at the guard opposite him. They glanced toward each other, and Arianna muttered, "Bet I get a cleaner shot than you."

"You're on, Lawson," he murmured. "Stay close."

Shots fired from each rifle, the sound echoing through the air before each guard clasped a knee cap, screaming before falling to the ground. They writhed in pain as they each gripped their bleeding legs.

"That will keep them down for a bit," Arianna yelled, jogging toward the left side of the lab entrance. "Come on."

Dominic ran to the right flank, both of them taking out the two remaining guards on each side before approaching the front door. After yanking the badge from the writhing guard's neck, she swiped it through the reader that would unlock the door.

"You fucking bitch!" the guard screamed, lifting his handgun as he still clung to his knee with his other hand. Grunting, Arianna kicked him in the face with her boot. His body went lax as he fell unconscious, and Dominic raised his eyebrows. "Nice kick. Does the badge work?"

Arianna swiped it again, her eyes widening with excitement when the little red dot turned from red to green. Pulling open the door, she turned and waved to Dani and Maverick.

Maverick shot Dani a quick nod, and she followed him as he jogged toward the lab. After ushering her inside, he began leading them down the darkened hallway.

"Stay alert," he commanded as Arianna and Dominic flanked them. "Although the lab is no longer functional, Cromwell knows we're coming, according to Tristan. There are cameras everywhere, and who knows who's watching on the other end?"

They rounded a corner, startling a guard who sat in a metal folding chair, head hung as he dozed. Lifting his head, he scrambled for his gun as Arianna held up her rifle. "Don't do it. I've got a clean shot between your eyes. Lower your gun and let us restrain you. Your choice."

The guard's eyes widened as his hand froze on the gun. Nostrils flared as he debated pulling the gun or following Arianna's command.

"You've got two seconds, buddy—"

"Okay," he said, lifting his hands. "Restrain me."

Dominic moved forward, jerking the guard's hands behind his back and tying them with the rope he'd secured on his belt. Instructing the guard to lie down on the concrete floor, he tied his ankles together, removed the man's duty belt and tossed it to the other side of the hallway.

"Come on," he said, jerking his head. "We're almost there."

They continued down the hallway, turning another corner. Dani gasped as she observed the lab before her, enclosed behind glass windows. It was expansive with rows of metal tables lined with all the equipment she would ever need to create plentiful stockpiles of antidote as well as her cancer vaccine. No wonder she'd been lured by the promise of working in the lab. So much opportunity, wasted because evil men wanted to profit on the pain of so many.

Shouts echoed in the distance, and Maverick faced Dominic and Arianna. "I've got four IEDs in my bag and one of the lighters." He patted his backpack. "You two hold off whoever that is so we can grab the antidote."

Arianna began to follow Dominic but turned to squeeze Dani's arm. "See you on the other side, sis. You've got this."

Dani smiled at the display of affection, which was rare from her stoic sister, and whispered, "I love you."

Arianna's lips formed a smile before she pivoted and followed Dominic down the hallway.

Facing her husband, Dani said, "I'm ready."

Covering his fist with a cloth, he punched through the glass door, spraying glass over the floor as he reached inside to grab the handle. Opening it, he ushered her inside. As she trailed through the rows of tables and equipment, something tingled in the far reaches of Dani's mind. The room felt so familiar, and as she glanced at the microscope across the room, she gasped.

"Dani?" Maverick asked, halting and grabbing her hand. "What is it?"

"I remember," she whispered, blood thrumming in her veins as she surveyed the room before staring into her husband's eyes. "I remember...champagne. Did we drink champagne in the lab?"

"Holy shit," he whispered, excitement flashing in his eyes. "We did, but I don't have time to tell you the story now." He tugged her hand, leading her to the secure area in the back of the room.

Once they arrived, he pointed to the pad on the side of the door. "This one needs your index fingerprint."

Lifting her finger, Dani touched the pad. A blue light scanned her finger before several beeps sounded. After a moment, the door clicked open.

"Fuck yes!" Maverick hissed, pushing open the door. Approaching the next door, he pointed at the keypad. "Any chance you remember the ten-digit code since you remember the champagne?"

Massaging her temples, Dani willed herself to remember, but her brain was fogged. "I can't. I'm sorry."

"It's okay. Stand back." Slinging his pack off his back, he pulled out the four IEDs, placing the small containers at the bottom of the door. "This will be loud and alert everyone to our presence. Plug your ears and crouch outside the first door. I'm going to light it, let it blow and then we'll head inside and grab the antidote."

Nodding furiously, Dani followed his orders, stepping back outside and crouching down to hold her ears. The silence was deafening as she waited with bated breath, anticipating the blow. Maverick appeared at her side, lowering beside her before the ground shook. Rising on shaky feet, she followed him back to the door, waving away the smoke as it cleared.

"Okay, you always said the antidote was stashed in a biomedical storage container in this room," he said, pushing open the crumbled door and leading her inside the dark room. "I know nothing about biomedical storage, so this is all you, Dani."

Allowing her eyes to adjust to the dim light, she observed the rows of cylindrical containers. Walking toward the first row, she unlatched the lid and lifted it as a cloud of cold air puffed from inside.

"They're refrigerated," she said, lowering the container when she found it empty. "There must be a different stash. I don't think I would've created an antidote that required refrigeration. It would make it less accessible. We need to find the room temperature storage area."

"How about there?" he asked, pointing to a metal door with a biohazard sign.

"Yes," she said, inching forward. "I wonder if there's a lock..." Feeling the cool metal, she inserted her fingers in the metal ring, drawing it back and tugging. "I think it's stuck." Grunting, she gripped harder and pulled.

"Let me try." Maverick clenched the ring attached to the door, muscles flexing as he yanked. It flew open, revealing a square cabinet built into the wall. Approaching it, Dani grasped the handle and opened the cabinet drawer.

Peering inside, she spotted a white box with a biohazard symbol on top. Reaching inside, she peeled open the lid to find ten vials full of milky liquid. "This is it," she said. "It has to be."

Reaching with both hands, she palmed the box, halting when she heard a *thunk* behind her. Rotating, she saw Maverick fall to the ground, unconscious. Sinking into a surreal dream that was rapidly becoming a nightmare, Dani slowly turned to face the woman holding a crowbar high, ready to strike.

Chapter 27

D ominic heard the sound of boots smacking the hard floor and knew the Sen Force reinforcements were on the way. Arianna jogged beside him, back toward the entrance, and he was thankful she was with him. If they had to fight to the death, he'd relish having her by his side.

They crested the corner, meeting a flurry of bullets before Dominic grabbed her arm and tugged her back into an adjoining hallway. Panting from exertion, he said, "I spotted at least five."

"That's how many I saw," she said, drawing the rifle from behind her shoulder so it hung above her abdomen, ready to be fired. Retrieving her handgun, she cocked it, the movement firm and sure. "I'll attack from left to right and you'll do the opposite."

He nodded, acknowledging their agreed tactical method. Since she was left handed, the strategy gave them the best odds. "I think we need to shoot to kill on this one."

"Fuckers. I know. The vests the guards outside wore left a small opening in the neck. Go for that or the head."

"I'd chide you for bossing me around, but we don't have time."

Her eyes lifted to his, green flecks sparkling in her hazel irises, and she grabbed his sleeve before twisting the fabric. "Don't die. You hear me?"

A small hum ignited in every cell as he stared down at her, wishing he could stop time. Why was her gaze so intense? It was as if he felt her energy wrapping around him, and it was shifting something profound and deep each millisecond.

"Ari—"

"Let's go."

Releasing the fabric, she inhaled a deep breath before charging forward. Dominic followed her, determined to protect Dani and Maverick in the lab, but also to protect Arianna. There had been something in those limitless eyes he needed to explore, and he'd damn well do it once they were safe.

They surged into the oncoming onslaught, Dominic thankful for the bulletproof vests he'd packed when he originally went on the run. They wouldn't protect every part of their bodies, but they were better than nothing.

Lifting his gun, he squinted one eye, aiming at the guard on the far right and shooting him in the forehead. He fell, causing the guard beside him to trip over his body, and Dominic lodged a bullet in that man's throat. Arianna took out two guards on the left, leaving only one rushing toward them.

Holstering her handgun, Arianna lifted the rifle, unloading a spray of bullets into the man's chest. Before he fell, he discharged one final round and fell to the floor.

Air jetted from Dominic's lungs, and he lifted his hand to his neck, palming the area of his skin that had somehow exploded. Sucking in deep breaths, he realized he was inhaling his own blood. Feeling his eyelids droop, his legs collapsed beneath him and he fell to the ground.

"No!" Arianna screamed, slinging the rifle behind her back and crouching beside him. Resting on her knees, her hands patted his chest before she drew his hand from his bleeding neck. "Fuck!" she cried, pressing her palm to the gushing wound as Dominic choked on his blood. "You're hit."

His lips moved, unable to form words as her arms moved furiously above him. Removing the rifle, she set it on the floor and yanked off her shirt, the expanse of her smooth skin glowing around her black sports bra. Balling her shirt, she pressed it to his wound, the pressure causing Dom to howl in pain.

"I know it hurts. We have to stop the bleeding. Can you breathe? Damn it, Dom. I need you to breathe." Pulling him to a sitting position, she pushed his back against the cinderblock wall, opening his airway a bit as she held compression. "That should help."

Dominic saw something over her shoulder. Just a tiny blip as someone passed between the hallways in the distance. Was it Raquel? No, it couldn't be. They'd left her in the woods, right? Overcome with pain, Dominic's mind was muddled as he tried to retain consciousness.

"Someone's...here..." he sputtered, attempting to point toward where he'd seen the flash. "Have to go to Dani and Mav. Trouble..."

"I can't leave you here," she said, her voice more erratic than he'd ever heard. Arianna was always so composed. So infallible. But now, as he felt the life dripping from his bones, he saw the emotion she kept buried deep inside.

"Ari," he whispered, lifting his bloody hand to cup her cheek. "Can't...save...me. Go..."

A sob tore from her throat as she shook her head. Her chin trembled as she maneuvered the shirt, pressing it tighter against his skin.

"It's okay..."

"Dominic..." Emotion swirled in her eyes, laced with such agony he longed to draw it from her. Squeezing her jaw, he silently urged her to leave him.

Staring deep into his eyes, she shook her head, her gaze unblinking as she let him finally see her. Past all the walls and the suppressed emotion, Dominic finally understood why she hated him so vehemently.

Because it wasn't hate after all. Arianna Lawson's brilliant orbs gazed at him, filled with all the unrequited love she felt for him and he'd never even thought to give her. What a waste. All this time, he'd hidden behind a false love for Dani to protect himself when Arianna had been beside him the entire time. And now, he was going to die before he could do a damn thing about it.

"You can't die," she rasped through clenched teeth, shaking her head as she pressed the shirt to his neck. "You son of a bitch, if you die, I'm going to murder you myself. Do you fucking hear me?"

Dominic tried to laugh at the nonsensical words, although the sound was garbled by the blood mixed with the air in his throat. Moving his hand to hers atop the compress, he tried to tug it away. "I'll hold...you go... Dani needs you..."

Pain flashed in her eyes, and he wanted to kick himself, knowing she interpreted his statement as yet another avowal of love for her sister. If he only had more time, he'd tell her he hadn't known. Hadn't even fathomed she cared for him. That his love for Dani had been a shield because he was too scared to love again.

That, for her, if they had just a bit more time, he might be willing to try.

Cursing the fates that led them here, he slumped to the floor, unable to support the weight of his body any longer.

"Hold this tight," she said, leaning over him as he rested on his back. "I'll be back soon." Leaning forward until their noses grazed, she gritted one last time, "Don't. Fucking. Die. I mean it, you son of a bitch." Closing her eyes, she rested her forehead against his for a moment that lasted an eternity. Then, she rose, slung her rifle back over her shoulder and ran to help her sister.

Chapter 28

Dani's mouth fell open as she observed her husband unconscious on the ground. Furious heartbeats clamored in her chest as she slowly lifted her gaze. Focusing on eyes similar to her own, a sob escaped her lips as her legs threatened to collapse. Betrayal, thick and suffocating, circulated through her veins as she worked her jaw, unable to speak due to the pervasive shock.

"You really should've trusted your little notes, Dani," Raquel said, her tone menacing as she held the crowbar high. "Now Maverick's down for the count, and I'm sorry to say, you're next."

"How did you get here?" Dani asked, shock pervading her veins.

"I'm not an idiot, contrary to what you all think," she spat. "I found a car nearby and hotwired it as soon as you left. Pretty resilient for your boring little sister, huh?" she taunted, rapidly blinking as she smirked.

Pain speared through Dani's brain, and she pressed her palms to her temples as a memory surged deep within. *The sound of sirens blaring as Sendaxa ordered everyone out of the lab. Rushing to this very room to retrieve the antidote. Hearing someone behind her and whirling to see who it was...*

She'd assumed it was a guard, even though she heard Raquel's voice in the background too...and she'd turned to find her sister, standing in the same position she was now...holding a crowbar high before slamming it down on her head.

"You were the one who hit me!" Dani exclaimed, outraged and heartbroken at her sister's betrayal. "Why would you do that?"

Scoffing, Raquel's eyes filled toxic rage, causing anguish to churn in Dani's gut. "Because you're so fucking *perfect*, right, Dani? Why would anyone hurt you?"

"I don't understand," she said, extending her hands. "I love you, Raquel—"

"Shut up!" Advancing forward, Raquel lifted the crowbar higher. "Just shut the fuck up. You've taken from me my entire life and relished having me in your shadow. That ends today. I'm going to be the one who leaves here with the antidote, and I'm going to *finally* earn something on my own for once."

"What the hell are you talking about?"

"You just couldn't let me have *anything*, could you?" Her chin warbled, showing a brief moment of indecision. "I didn't want to hurt you, Dani, but you just can't get out of my way."

"I don't understand—"

"The job here?" She gestured with her hand. "I applied and was more than qualified, but no, you had to swoop in and meddle to make sure I got it. It was the same thing when I applied at Columbia. You just can't help yourself."

"I was trying to help you!" Dani said, exasperated. "I want the best for you, Raquel. I always have."

"Have you?" Arching a brow, she inched closer. "Because you took the final moments I'd ever have with her, and you didn't even care. Why would you? You always thought yourself so fucking important. So much better than me."

Dani struggled to understand her cryptic words. "With Mom?"

"Yes, with Mom," she hissed. "Arianna got to say goodbye, and then you went in after her. You were only supposed to stay a few minutes, but you lingered because you thought your goodbye was more important than mine. Who needed to say goodbye to the ugly, imperfect daughter? The afterthought? You created that role for me and I hate it! You've kept me in a gilded cage, and I won't live in your shadow anymore."

Tears burned Dani's eyes as she regarded the person she loved more than anyone in the world, along with Arianna. Her sisters were her rocks, and her mind was struggling to process the intense hatred in Raquel's green eyes. Swiping away a tear, she emitted a soft sob. "All along, it was you who gave me amnesia."

"Yes. My plan was to steal the antidote and take it to the District to make a deal with Luthor Cromwell. They had just started to wall off the cities, and I knew he would need scientists. This time, I could secure my *own* future."

"But he's evil, Raquel—"

"I don't think you have any room to point fingers," she said, arching a brow. "After all, you're the one who created this disaster. I tried to tell you the EverLife formula would be too addictive. You were so sure the poppy extracts wouldn't be a problem. So sure that people would stick to the recommended dose. Your optimism has always been your downfall."

"Did you know that Sendaxa falsified the clinical trial data?"

Malicious laughter exited her throat. "For god's sake, Dani, wake up! Sendaxa is the most powerful company in the world, and EverLife was a goldmine. Of course I knew. They paid off the FDA regulators and sent it into full production. The consumers never stood a chance."

Shaking the crowbar, Raquel's lips formed a nefarious smile. "Look at me. You never once believed your frumpy little sister could harm you. I knew eventually we'd end up here again, but this time, I'm not going to fail."

"You pushed me into the pitchfork," Dani accused softly.

"You'd had a flashback that day of seeing me in the lab with something in my hands." Shaking the crowbar, she smirked. "We got in an argument and I pushed you. I didn't mean to ram you into a pitchfork, but it certainly came in handy."

A warbled cry leapt from her throat. "Are you going to kill me? God, Raquel, do you hate me that much?"

"I have no wish to kill you," she murmured, a small flare of emotion contorting her features. "I just want to be free of you and all the painful memories I have because of you. It's time for me to have my turn as the one everyone reveres. The one who inspires greatness."

"Please, Raquel," Dani pleaded, holding up her hands. "I never meant to hurt you. I didn't realize your feelings about Mom's goodbye, but I should have. I'm so sorry."

"I never wanted to hurt you either," she said, stepping forward. "Unfortunately, I've learned the hard way we never get what we want in life unless we take it." Lifting the weapon, Raquel snarled as her arms began to swing.

Dani crossed her arms in front of her face, turning to try and escape the blow. And then, everything went black as she fell to the ground.

Chapter 29

Arianna ran to the main hub of the lab, more concerned with finding Dani, grabbing the antidote and returning to Dominic than anything else. Their interaction last night played in a constant loop in her brain, and she hoped to hell it wasn't the last cognizant conversation they would ever have. She'd stormed off like a petulant child. Now, she vowed to treat him differently if he survived. Hell, he couldn't control his feelings for Dani. Moreover, she'd never given him a reason to try. Frustrated with her emotional ineptitude, she charged over the broken glass, entering the lab as it crunched beneath her boots.

Approaching the thick metal doors, she stepped through the first one and noticed the second one blown apart by the IEDs. Drawing her handgun, she stepped over the threshold. Confusion marred her features as she tilted her head.

"Raquel?"

"Don't come any closer!" her sister yelled, whirling as she held a crowbar high. "They're both unconscious and I don't want to hurt them. But if you force me to, I'll slam this so hard on Dani's temple, it will crack in half before you shoot me." She shook the weapon, and Arianna noticed her hands were trembling quite fiercely. Arianna judged her words an empty threat, but she had no desire to shoot Raquel, despite her treachery. Something awful must've prompted her actions, and Arianna would always give her sisters the benefit of the doubt.

But just because she didn't want to hurt her didn't mean she wasn't pissed as hell. "What the fuck, Raquel? You don't have to do this."

"No, I don't," she said, lifting her chin. "I could choose to remain someone no one sees and live an uneventful life. But I'm choosing another path."

"You're not going to best me when I'm holding this and you've got a crowbar," Arianna said, shaking the gun. "You know this, Raquel."

"That's where you're wrong, I'm afraid," a deep baritone said behind her. The sound of a gun cocking beside her ear caused Arianna to freeze. Ice coursed through her veins as she debated turning to see who was behind her.

"Well, little mouse," the man droned, "you've certainly surprised me. Luthor Cromwell has plans for what needs to happen in this lab, and you're fucking it up. But I admire your spunk, so I'm going to help you."

"I'm not working with you!" Raquel cried. "I'm stealing the antidote and heading to the District, where I'm going to approach Cromwell. I'll be able to replicate it when I have access to technology inside the wall and I can create a better lite version than he's using now."

The man hesitated, and Arianna took the moment to spin and point her gun in his face. Tossing back his head, he laughed before shrugging. "Go ahead. Shoot me. But I'll shoot her first." He pointed the gun at Raquel. Arianna stood firm, calculating in her mind how long it would take to shoot him and then shoot to wound Raquel.

"I assume you're Tristan Holder. Thanks for the weapons, by the way." Arianna arched a sardonic eyebrow. "*Really* helpful."

"You're welcome," he said with an arrogant nod. "I needed you to end up here. I didn't count on *her* though," he said, gesturing to Raquel with his gun. "And if you don't drop your weapon, I'll shoot her."

Arianna stood firm, continuing to calculate in her mind. Something flared in Tristan's eyes before he lowered the gun and aimed at Dani, who was unconscious on the floor. "Or maybe I'll shoot her."

"Okay," Arianna said, lowering the gun and holstering it before showing her palms. No way was she going to take a chance with Dani and Maverick lying unconscious and no ability to even try to avoid a shot.

"Seriously?" Raquel squeaked. "You didn't care when he was going to shoot me, but of course you care about Dani. I hate you as much as I hate her right now."

"As much as I love this family drama," Tristan said with an exasperated eye roll, "we've got to go. Raquel, grab the antidote and come with me."

"I don't trust you—"

"You don't really have a choice. It's me or the people you just betrayed."

Raquel hesitated and he shrugged. "Fine, have it your way." He aimed the gun at her and Arianna screamed, "No!"

"Okay!" Raquel said, tossing the crowbar to the ground. Reaching inside, she grabbed the box with the antidote and approached Tristan. "Let's go."

Keeping his weapon trained on Arianna, he backed out of the room, ushering Raquel to go ahead of him. "I have a first aid kit in the car. Probably won't help Dominic, but it's better than nothing. I'll leave it on the north end of the lot."

"I'm *really* fucking confused. Now you want to help Dom?"

"There are things in play here that need to happen. I'm not interested in all this." He circled his hand. "I'm interested in starting a war. And that won't happen until Cromwell gets the video footage he needs of Dani. He has a vision of painting her as a villain. I have two men waiting outside, and I'll tell them you escaped but you have to go now. There's a back door emergency exit at the end of the secondary hallway. Use that instead of the front entrance."

Retreating, he gave a mischievous grin. "Oh, and one more thing. There's a false bottom in the drawer where Dani hid the antidote. Make sure you check there before you leave."

"How in the hell do you know that?"

"I make it my business to know things, Arianna. Now hurry the fuck up." Giving a nod, he rotated and fled to catch up with Raquel, who'd already disappeared.

A moan sounded and Arianna turned to find Dani wiggling on the ground as she cupped her head. "What the hell?" she groaned.

"Raquel hit you," Arianna explained, rushing over. "Long story. Mav's unconscious. Let me try to wake him." Rushing over, she crouched and turned him to splay on his back. Slapping his cheek several times, she called his name.

Suddenly, his eyes flew open and he gasped. Sitting up, he shook his head rapidly as if trying to clear it. "What the fuck happened?"

"I actually remember," Dani said, rubbing the back of her head. "Raquel hotwired a car and showed up with a crowbar. Jesus, my head is pounding."

"Dominic was hit," Arianna said, pointing to the door. "I have to get back to him. Tristan said he'd leave a first aid kit in the parking lot."

"Tristan Holder?" Maverick asked, confused.

"Yeah. Lots to catch up on. Can you two manage while I go retrieve Dom? Tristan said to exit through the back emergency exit so his men don't see us."

"Go," Maverick said, shooing her as he scooted toward Dani. "We'll help each other."

"There's a false bottom in the drawer. Check it." Rising, Arianna broke into a sprint toward the front of the lab, racing toward the man she loved while praying it wasn't too late to save him.

Once Maverick and Dani gained their bearings, they stood and searched the cabinet. Finding the false bottom, they lifted the top, and Dani breathed a sigh of relief when she saw the two vials inside.

"Well, it's not a full box, but it will have to do." Retrieving them, she walked back to the lab and located two cloths, carefully wrapping both vials before placing them in her bag. Rushing from the lab, they found Arianna dragging Dominic down the hallway toward the back exit.

Dani observed his shallow breathing and lowered to take his pulse. "Pulse is faint, but it's there and he's breathing. Maverick, can you carry him?"

"I'll help," Arianna said, her face a mask of concern. Sliding her arms under his knees, she gathered him in her arms as Maverick lifted him under his chest. They carried him through the back exit and through the woods to the truck. Dani jogged toward them, extending the first aid kit.

"Found it on the edge of the parking lot."

Maverick and Dani assessed the wound as Dominic lay in the bed of the truck, concern lacing their features.

"It was a clean shot and I think we can manage the bleeding with constant pressure," Dani said. "But we also need to keep moving. The silver lining is that he's unconscious, which means he's not feeling pain."

"I'll continue to apply pressure as you drive," Arianna said, crawling in beside him and cradling him in her lap. Pressing a clean shirt to his wound, she gently stroked his short hair as his head rested in her lap. It was a poignant gesture, so different from her sister's gruff exterior, and Dani felt the curtain of realization lift as she nodded.

Climbing in the passenger seat, she massaged her throbbing head as Maverick drove. Once they were speeding down the open road, he reached over and clutched her hand. "You okay? Besides the pounding in your skull that probably rivals mine?"

"I'm fine," she said, stunned as she recalled Arianna's soft strokes on Dominic's head. "Ari's in love with Dominic," she whispered.

Maverick's eyes narrowed. "What makes you say that? They barely tolerate each other."

"That's Arianna's love language," she said, breathing a laugh. "The verbal quips and zingers. It's always been how she communicates."

"I'll be damned," he mused. "I won't deny I've noticed the energy between them. It's fucking intense."

"I hope he's okay." Gripping the window frame, she watched the fields zip by. "Did we fail, Maverick?"

"Not yet. Let's find a place to camp, regroup and get some rest. We haven't failed yet, sweetheart."

Gripping his hand, she drew upon his strength as he drove them far away from the lab.

Chapter 30

They found a clearing in a thicket of woods, the canopy of trees a perfect shield from the outside world. They took turns sleeping around the fire Arianna built, continuing to wake each other to ensure they monitored any concussions. Dani used the meager tools in Tristan's first aid kit and stitched up Dominic with the needle and thread she'd packed from the farmhouse. They'd each packed random trinkets and supplies they thought might come in handy, and Dani was thankful she'd thought to toss them in.

She'd also packed the antibiotic ointment and made sure to slather it on Dominic's stitches when she was finished. His pulse was stronger as he slept, which was promising. Once the sun rose, they decided to stay another day as Dani and Maverick took the ibuprofen Dani had also stashed. After two days, they felt it was time to move.

Tristan had also left a SIM card in the first aid kit, which Arianna studied by the fire. "Ready to see what's on here? We have seventy-five percent battery on the phone but need to use it sparingly since we don't have the generator to charge it anymore and Dani still needs to watch the videos each morning."

Maverick inserted the SIM card. After the information loaded, he pulled up a series of images. Studying them, his eyes grew wide. "Tristan supplied us with maps of all the known black-market compounds. And he made a list of the leaders with detailed instructions of which ones we should approach first."

"And?" Arianna asked.

"This one," he said, showing them the screen. "It's in Cumberland, Maryland, near the border of Pennsylvania."

"We have enough gas to get there?" Dani asked.

Maverick nodded. "The leader is supposedly a former US senator named Arthur Reyes."

"I remember that name," Dani said. "Wasn't he mulling a run for president? He was a centrist who was popular with both political parties, right?"

Maverick and Arianna's mouths fell open as they gaped at her.

"What is it?"

"Sweetheart, Arthur Reyes rose to prominence *after* you started working at Sendaxa."

"Holy shit," she whispered, rubbing her forehead. "I remember him...I remember his popularity."

"Dani, do you remember our wedding?"

Gazing into his eyes, her lips ticked down as she shook her head. "I don't remember that. I'm so sorry—"

"That's okay," he said, inching closer and pulling her into his arms. "You remember something and that's amazing."

"Maybe my memories are going to return in a slow drip as I heal." Rubbing her head, she shot him a derisive look. "I mean, getting hit again certainly didn't help."

"Maybe it knocked things right again," Arianna interjected.

Laughing, Dani lifted a shoulder. "Maybe."

Maverick held her, rocking them back and forth as Arianna leaned over to check Dominic's wound. "We need to leave this site tomorrow. We can find a new camp along the way."

"Agreed. We'll take it day by day and approach Reyes's compound when we're stronger."

"Hopefully, we can find an abandoned school nearby and use their lab. We'll need one with a generator so I have electricity. Then, I'm going to figure out what I put in this antidote and replicate the shit out of it."

The conversation continued well into the night before they all took turns keeping watch so they could sleep.

Tristan stood in Luthor Cromwell's office, lurking in the corner as Raquel waited in the center of the expansive room. Luthor stood off to the side, slowly sipping one of the deep brown scotches he kept in the fancy crystal decanters that lined the bar. Tossing back his glass, he chugged the final drops before setting it down and approaching Raquel.

"Well, my dear, you were certainly a curveball we didn't foresee," he said in his raspy voice. Tilting his head, he studied her like a bug under a microscope. "You almost ruined my plans. I needed the footage of your sister breaking into the lab and attempting to steal the antidote. I plan to show it as proof of her treachery during her public trial. It will garner support for me as I continue to build a new government under the Sendaxa umbrella."

"I...I'm sorry," Raquel said, knuckles white as she clenched the box that held the antidote. "I had my own plans, and I finally gained the courage to enact them."

"Tristan assures me I shouldn't hunt Dani down yet. That I should use the footage to convince people she's trying to resume production of EverLife and harm others. No one knows she was trying to steal the antidote. What do you think, my dear?"

Her throat bobbed as she rapidly blinked several times. "It's always better to write your own narrative. I see the logic in that argument."

"I agree." Extending his palms, he waited, urging her along. She placed the box in his hands and he opened it, his thin lips forming a sinister grin as he gazed inside. "You say you can create a new antidote that will extend the effects of EverLife?"

Nodding, she lifted her face to his, causing a jolt of admiration to shoot down Tristan's spine. Her expression was clear and rather confident for someone who was standing in front of the most powerful—and most evil—man in the world.

"I can make an antidote that will dull the EverLife side effects but cause the body to retain the cravings. It will create a need for EverLife so great I can't see anyone who's addicted stopping."

"Constant consumption," he drawled, pleasure in his tone. "A product no one can live without. It will give Sendaxa ultimate power."

"Sendaxa is already powerful," Tristan muttered, unable to stop himself. "How much more do you need?"

"If I want your opinion, I'll ask for it, Tristan," Luthor scolded, his expression stern. Clenching his jaw, Tristan forced himself to remain quiet. The two bodyguards along the wall pierced him with their gazes, and he glowered at them, suppressing the urge to flip the bastards off.

Resettling his attention on Raquel, Luthor slipped his fingers under her chin, tilting her face to his. She was almost a foot shorter than Luthor, and something protective welled in his chest as the wicked man loomed over her. Although she'd concocted an illicit secret plan to dupe her sister, Raquel wasn't a soldier, nor did she truly understand how evil someone like Luthor could be.

She was much like his sister had been before she'd fallen under Luthor's clutches. Tristan hadn't been able to save Jessica, but he could sure as hell keep Raquel from being drawn into Luthor's inner circle. Perhaps saving her would bring him some peace to counteract his abject failure with Jessica.

"I assume you'll need shelter," Luthor continued, a sinister gleam entering his eyes as he held her chin. "Of course, you will have to *earn* your place here. I don't appreciate freeloaders."

"I told you, I will work on the antidote and anything else you require." She stepped back, pulling away from his grasp. "Surely that's payment enough. I'm a very competent scientist and worked with my sister for years in Bethesda. I have knowledge that will benefit you."

"That will pay for your food and clothing," he said, leaning his hip against the nearby desk, "but lodging is a separate matter. I have several apartments I could offer, but they will require other forms of restitution."

"She can stay with me," Tristan blurted before he even felt the words pass his lips. "It will allow me to gather intel on her sister and their team, and monitor Raquel as she works. I'm still not sure we can trust her. Her sister could've planted her here to destroy us from the inside. We can't be certain."

"I assure you, I am not a spy," Raquel said, glaring at him.

Tristan glowered back, attempting to inform her with his gaze to shut her mouth before she said something that made it impossible for him to save her from the vile man.

Her eyes widened a bit as understanding dawned, and she turned to face Luthor. "But I can see why you might be suspicious. I'm happy to stay with Tristan if it will calm your doubts."

Luthor's eyes traveled over her body, raking over her curves in the baggy clothes as if he were considering a mare for breeding. Finally, he waved a dismissive hand. "Fine. Stay with Tristan so he can keep an eye on you. I will require regular reporting about how the new antidote is progressing."

"Yes, sir," Raquel said.

"Go on, then," Luthor said, dismissing them as he stalked behind his desk. "I have a ton of video footage to sift through and manipulate to ensure Dani looks as guilty as possible from the break-in. Tristan, you'll take Raquel to the lab tomorrow morning and get her situated?"

"Yes." Stepping forward, he gripped her forearm. "Come on."

Yanking away, she shot him a hateful glare. "I can walk on my own, thank you." She strode ahead of him, out of the office and into the elevator as Tristan entered behind her. Once the doors whooshed shut and they began the descent to the lobby, Tristan hit the emergency button, halting them in between floors.

"What are you doing?" she gasped, clutching the walls.

Stepping forward, he tried to talk some sense into her obstinate little head. "You listen to me, little mouse. I just saved you from having that old man's dick shoved between your lips for the rest of your days here. He's a monster, and you'll do well to remember that."

Her mouth fell open, shock covering every inch of her expression, and he had to tame the urge to laugh. Whether she liked it or not, she was about to get a dose of the harsh reality she'd entered.

"You hate your sister, but at least her motives were pure. You won't find purity here." He pointed at the closed doors. "All you'll find is a madman intent on destroying what's left of the world. I aim to fix that, and because I'm a nice fucking guy, I'm going to save your ass too."

"I do not need saving from the likes of you, and I would appreciate it if you stopped screaming in my face!"

"Don't test me," he said, leaning closer. "I feel an urge to protect you, but my goodwill only extends so far. You're a smart woman—much wilier than I gave you credit for—so you'll understand this in time: I'm your only ally here. If you're as intelligent as I think you are, you'll accept that and work *with* me instead of against me. Are we clear?"

"Yes," she whispered as a fear swirled in her eyes.

"Good." Drawing back, he punched the elevator button, resuming their trip to the lobby. When they exited, Tristan cursed as his ex-wife sauntered toward them.

"Oh, I...uh, hello, Tristan," Grace said, eyebrows drawn together as she assessed Raquel.

"Grace," he said with a curt nod.

"Hello," she said, extending her hand. "I'm Grace, Luthor Cromwell's wife."

"Raquel," she said, shaking her hand. "I'll be working for Luthor to improve the antidote distributed in the District."

"I see." Lifting her gaze to Tristan's, she released the woman's hand as her nostrils flared. "Raquel is a pretty name. Pleasure to meet you."

A muscle in Tristan's jaw clenched as he gazed into his ex-wife's eyes. For a fraction of a moment, they reflected the pain and heartache that simmered in his own. Then, the mask returned as Grace's expression turned blank.

"I wish you well," she said, stepping into the elevator and pressing the keypad. The doors whooshed shut as Tristan encircled Raquel's wrist.

"Come on," he ordered, leading her outside.

She stayed silent as they walked the ten blocks to his apartment. The small den had a pull-out couch, and he informed her it would be her room for the foreseeable future. After rummaging for some boxer shorts and a t-shirt, he tossed them on the bed before pointing to the half bath outside.

"You can use that for now. Do you need anything else?"

"I have supplies from the farmhouse in my bag," she said, sitting on the bed and swiping her thick brown hair off her forehead. "Been using the same toothbrush for a while, but I guess it's better than nothing."

"We can get supplies this week. Inflation is rampant inside the walls since our currency is from a government that no longer exists. It's become a wild west mentality of sorts. I assume Luthor will begin to print his own currency soon, which will exacerbate his power."

Those clear green eyes studied him as she gnawed her lip. "I can tell you don't like him. You must have your own plan to take him down. I'd love to hear it. Perhaps we can work together to see if our interests align."

Leaning against the doorframe, he narrowed his eyes. "I bet you'd love to hear it," he muttered. "I'm not interested in aligning with anyone. For some reason, I've decided I want to protect you, so let's leave it at that." Grasping the doorknob, he backed out of the room. "Good night, Raquel."

"Wait," she called, lifting her hand.

Sighing, he crossed his arms. "Yes?"

"The woman I met. Grace. You two have a history."

"Yes."

Nervously licking her lips, she smiled. "It was nice of her to comment on my name. My mom loved that name."

Tristan's heart squeezed in his chest, sure as if a fist had reached inside his chest and crushed it. "We loved it too."

"We?"

"Grace and I. It was the name we picked for our daughter."

"Oh." Raquel's eyes lit with curiosity. "Is she...?"

He shook his head. "Grace lost the baby when she was five months pregnant."

A ragged breath escaped Raquel's lips. "I'm so sorry."

"Thank you. As I said, I have a compelling urge to protect you. Perhaps I'm nostalgic because of your name. Regardless, it's important to remember you're never safe in this fucked-up world. I'll do my best, but you need to be smart and alert."

Nodding, she straightened her shoulders. "I understand. Thank you, Tristan."

"You're welcome. Good night."

Striding up the stairs to his room, Tristan yanked off his clothes, crawling into bed as exhaustion set in. Harshly rubbing his eyes, he wondered how in the hell he'd ended up with a stowaway scientist. That definitely hadn't been in his plans, but now that she was here, he'd do his best to keep her safe.

Closing his eyes, he thought of Jessica. And then of Grace. And eventually, about the baby they'd lost so long ago. Sighing, he switched off the lamp, understanding he needed sleep so he could forge ahead when the sun rose.

Chapter 31

The team arrived at the Cumberland, Maryland, black-market compound on fumes, causing Dani to breathe a sigh of relief. She and Maverick exited the truck, leaving Arianna in the back with Dominic. He'd awoken that morning in severe pain, and Dani had urged him to rest. She hoped they could get their hands on better medical supplies if Arthur Reyes allowed them inside the compound.

Approaching the tall wooden doors, Maverick lifted his fist and pounded. A voice yelled from behind, "Who goes there?"

"My name is Maverick Ward. I was the head of security at the Sendaxa lab where EverLife was created. My wife, Danica, is with me, and we want to speak to Arthur Reyes."

Muffled voices sounded behind the door before a deep voice called, "It will be a few minutes."

He and Dani waited, glancing ever so often at Arianna and Dominic in the bed of the truck several feet away. Finally, the huge doors swung open, and a man with a rifle slung over his back stepped outside. Several men flanked him, all armed, and Maverick showed his palms.

"I have a gun on my belt, but you're welcome to confiscate it. We come in peace."

The leader gestured with his head, and one of his soldiers stepped forward to frisk Maverick and remove his gun. He also frisked Dani before returning to the leader and handing him the firearm. "They're both clear."

Placing the gun in his belt, the man regarded them under the bright morning sky.

"You're Arthur Reyes?" Maverick asked.

"Yes." His eyes trailed to Dani. "And you're the woman who destroyed the world."

Dani squared her shoulders before nodding. "I am. There is no excuse, so I won't try to make one. All I can say is that I will work until my dying breath to repair the damage. I have two vials of antidote, and if you'll help me find a warehouse or an abandoned school with any sort of science lab, I can figure out how to replicate it and begin to save people."

His eyes narrowed as his nostrils flared. "Can you bring back my sister, who died from the meaningless addiction she formed to your despicable drug?"

Dani's shoulders hunched as she shook her head. "I can't and I'm sorry. I know this doesn't mean anything, but my intentions were good. I never meant to create something that would harm so many."

"And yet you did" was his ominous reply. "Perhaps we should drag you inside and place you on trial for your transgressions."

"Hey," Maverick said, holding up his hands, "we came here in peace, Reyes, and I'm not above killing anyone who tries to harm my wife. There's a very capable soldier in that truck"—he pointed over his shoulder with his thumb—"who's ready to rush toward me, throw a rifle in my hand, and blast all of you full of bullets—"

"You're threatening me?" Reyes asked, cocking a brow. "You are aware I'm surrounded by ten armed guards, right?" He gestured toward his men.

"Fuck this," Maverick said, turning toward the truck to summon Arianna.

"Wait," Dani said, clutching his wrist and squeezing to calm him. Facing Reyes, she straightened her shoulders. "My husband has a protective streak, but he means no harm. And you're right. I should die for my crimes, and I'm willing to face the consequences of my actions. But first, I'd like to use my skills to try and help the ones who remain."

Dani stepped toward Reyes as Maverick gripped her arm to halt her. "No, Mav," she said, gently removing his hand. "I need to face this, and you need to let me."

His eyes pulsed with concern, but he finally released her. Stepping forward, she stopped when she was mere inches from Arthur Reyes. "I have amnesia and don't remember much about the past few years, although flashes of memory are slowly returning. One thing I do remember is your kindness and your involvement in a plethora of community activities benefiting so many. You were an activist before I royally fucked up and ruined everything. I'm asking you to let me help you so you can help others again. After that, I will surrender to your soldiers and you can put me on trial."

Reyes's eyes narrowed as he contemplated. "You're willing to die for your crimes?"

"Yes," she said, her tone firm. "But not before I repair the damage. That is something I can't live with...and I can't die knowing I didn't try. I hope you can understand."

Rubbing his chin with his fingers, he pondered. "I didn't expect you to be noble. Luthor Cromwell paints a terrible picture of you that has disseminated to all the black-market compounds."

"I would argue that Cromwell is the villain here. Perhaps I was a pawn, and an unwitting one at that, but I'll take responsibility." She gestured toward Maverick. "My husband, his best friend and my sister make up our small team. We could've stayed hidden and survived on our own. Instead, I'm here, asking you to let me make things right. I want you to judge me by my future actions, not the actions of my past." Reaching toward him, she covered his forearm. "And I'm very sorry about your sister," she rasped, emotion in her voice as her eyes clouded with tears. "I can't imagine the pain of losing her. When I lost my mother to cancer, I thought I might drown in grief. I'm just...well, I'm sorry, Arthur."

Releasing him, she stepped back, willing and waiting for whatever decision he wished to render. Finally, his features softened, and his lips formed the barest hint of a smile.

"Thank you for your condolences. She was a wonderful woman. Vibrant and full of life."

"I'd love to hear her story. She deserves that. All the victims of this senseless crisis do."

Inhaling a deep breath, Reyes lifted his gaze to Maverick. "Either your wife is very genuine or she's a great actress."

"I assure you, she's a terrible actress. If she doesn't like something or believe in it, she has no ability to hide her disapproval." His lips twitched as he gazed reverently toward Dani.

A low chuckle escaped Reyes's lips. "I think I believe you." Facing the man on his right, he asked, "We can put the four of them in the abandoned middle school on the northside of the compound. I believe it has all the remnants of a science lab and a generator, yes?"

"Yes, sir."

Turning to Dani, he asked, "Will that work?"

"If it's the best you've got, I'll take it," she said with a nod. "As long as we have a roof over our head, access to a lab and a generator, I'll work like hell to replicate the antidote. Do you have access to any facility with production capabilities?"

"There's an abandoned factory within the walls of our compound. It's no longer functional but can be resurrected with some effort, I would imagine."

"Good. Producing mass quantities of antidote is going to be difficult. Once I figure out what's in the formula, I'm going to need to tweak it to make it more natural so we don't rely on synthetic chemicals. Plants will need to be harvested to supply us with ingredients. It's a huge undertaking, but one worth executing."

"I appreciate the foresight. We're bare bones inside the walls. The school will have cots where you can sleep and a well in the back. There's a generator that can power your lab work."

"That will work," Maverick said.

Reyes nodded before pointing toward the entrance. "Drive your truck inside, and one of my men will drive you to the school. If it's empty, he can refill it along the way.

We've been sending out search parties to collect gas from abandoned vehicles and refueling stations."

"Thank you," Dani said, grateful for his acceptance. "I promise you, I'll do my best."

Arthur's eyes roved over her, clear and contemplative as he assessed. "My dear, I'm counting on it," he said before turning to step back into the compound.

Returning to the truck with Maverick, Dani climbed into the passenger seat and attempted to calm her pounding heart as they drove onto the compound.

Chapter 32

D ani observed the compound on the short drive to the school, noting the solemn atmosphere. Some houses had large red Xs sprayed on the front and boarded-up windows. Others were still habitable, and several children appeared as they neared the school. They ran alongside the truck until it stopped, and Dani stepped out to greet the kids.

"You're the bad woman who created EverLife," one of the children said, curiosity in his deep brown eyes as he studied her.

Dani nodded. "I am. I'm here to fix what I broke. Was this your school?"

"I wasn't old enough to go here yet. This was the middle school."

She cocked a brow. "I bet you can still show me around though. We need a place for my friend Dominic to rest. He's hurt and needs to recover."

The boy's gaze drifted to the back of the truck, where Arianna and Maverick were helping Dominic, who swayed on his feet as he slid to the ground. Arianna urged him to sling his arms over their shoulders before leading him toward the entrance.

"I can show you," the kid said, waving his hand. "Come on."

The driver Reyes had assigned tipped his ballcap before climbing back in the truck and driving away.

"Guess they're keeping the truck," Dani murmured as they followed the kids inside. She admired Reyes's confidence and acceptance, and felt a small well of gratitude that he was still alive. They would need altruistic, competent leaders for the huge undertaking ahead.

"You can put him there," the boy said, leading them through a doorway marked "infirmary" and pointing to the stretcher bed in the middle of the exam room.

"Perfect," Dani said, squeezing his shoulder. "Thank you..."

"Chris." His gap-toothed grin was adorable.

"You're a great helper, Chris. I'll remember that and might need your help again."

He gave a vigorous nod as Arianna and Maverick situated Dominic in the bed.

"You married?" Chris asked, pointing to Dominic.

"I'm actually married to that one," she said, tilting her head toward Maverick.

Chris's gaze drifted toward Arianna. "Is *she* married to him?"

"*Pfft*," Arianna said, backing away from the bed. "In his dreams. Is there another couch in this dump?"

"I can show you," one of the other kids chimed, and Arianna smiled before following the boy from the room.

"You two can sleep in the guidance counselor's office," Chris said. "It's two doors down, and the couch pulls out to a bed."

Dani leaned down and rested her hands on her knees to stare into his eyes. "Thank you, Chris. Maybe you can come back tomorrow and help us again? I think you're going to end up being a very valuable member of our team."

Biting his lip, he gave a quick nod before bolting from the room as the two remaining kids followed him.

Striding toward Dominic, Dani pressed her palm to his forehead. "He's still got a fever. Let me see what provisions they've got here. I'll clean and rebandage his wound."

"I'll go check on Arianna and scope out the guidance counselor's office," Maverick said, leaning down to kiss her cheek. "Come find me when you're done."

After he skirted from the room, Dani searched the cabinets, finding most of them empty. There were a few bandages, a bottle of hydrogen peroxide and some ibuprofen in a drawer, so she set them on the counter before shrugging off her pack. Retrieving the first aid kit, she stacked the contents on the counter and got to work.

She helped Dominic tug off his shirt before urging him to lie back so she could tend to his wound. It was ugly, but it would heal. Thank god. Losing Dominic would've wrecked her, and she needed to be in the right mindset to replicate the formula. Since she couldn't remember shit, she was going to have to study the antidote intensely, and needed to be focused.

"Arianna," Dominic whispered through chapped lips as Dani finished cleaning his wound.

"She needs some space," Dani said, opening a bandage and removing the adhesive covering.

Dominic's brown eyes darted between hers, laced with remorse and regret. "I didn't know," he rasped.

"Me neither." She pressed the bandage over his wound, lightly patting it in place. "She's not really a sharer."

Huffing a laugh, Dominic nodded against the pillow.

"She's going to fight it," Dani said, her lips forming a sad smile. "You know that, right?"

His Adam's apple bobbed as he nodded.

"You're both scared to love," she said, rising and retrieving the vial of petroleum jelly from the counter. "For different reasons, but they're all valid." After gathering some on her fingertip, she gently rubbed it over Dominic's lips to ease the chapping. "Don't let her push you away. She deserves love, Dom. She's never met a man worthy of her, nor someone who is strong enough to see past her walls and fight for her. I know you can do it. But let's get you better first, okay?"

His eyes drooped as his head barely moved in acknowledgment. Dani cupped his shoulder as he drifted to sleep. Rising, she made sure he was tucked in before she exited to find her husband.

Dani and Maverick decided to turn the guidance counselor's office into their bedroom. It offered privacy, and the pull-out couch was a bonus.

"Maybe the old counselor snuck in a nap or two when no one was looking?" Maverick teased as he arranged the bed.

"Maybe. Now that we're settled with sleeping quarters, we have a lot of tasks to complete to make this place functional so I can work."

There was no running water to the school, which Dani would need to remedy. In the meantime, Dani and Maverick washed off the grime of the day in the staid, multi-stalled bathroom next door with some of the water left in jugs by Arthur's men.

Once they were finally alone, situated in the pull-out bed, Dani slid her arms around her husband, thankful to have him by her side. Resting her cheek on his chest, she gently ran her fingers through the prickly hairs as they relaxed in the dark.

"Well, we made it to Phase II," she said, placing a sweet kiss on his pec. "We're really in it now."

"For better or worse," he said, sifting his hands through her hair as she nuzzled against him.

"The past few years were *definitely* worse," she droned, rolling her eyes. "But there were some good times before that. The times when you wore me down, even though I insisted we weren't right for each other." Resting her chin on his chest, she grinned. "That first time you told me you loved me, after we'd been dating for several months. You finally talked me into bed, and I hadn't been with anyone in a while. I figured I'd scratch an itch with you because having sex with someone as hot as you might never happen again. But you slid inside me, and threaded your fingers through mine, and told me you loved me. It was one of the most perfect moments of my life."

His eyes shimmered with wetness, unashamed, as he ran his fingers over her cheek. "You remember," he whispered, his tone reverent.

"I remember." Cupping his jaw, she traced her thumb over his lips. "I don't remember it all, but I remember enough to know this is real. I think I'll remember more each day, and hopefully, one day, I'll remember everything. The details of my work at Sendaxa and what happened there are still vague, but I remember you, Mav. How could I not?" Sliding to press a kiss on his lips, she straddled his thighs, longing to bring him inside her. "I love you."

"Dani," he breathed, searching for her...easing inside her once he was coated with her essence.

Staring deep into his eyes, she rode him, gliding over his sensitive skin, overcome with feeling.

"I've waited so long to hear you say it again. It was torture to tell you and not hear it back. I love you, sweetheart."

Pressing her palms to the mattress, she rose above him, undulating her hips to increase the pace. He whispered words of love, rising to meet her urgent thrusts as their skin heated with desire. Lowering her mouth to his, Dani surged her tongue inside, tasting the man who was her eternity.

His strong arms wrapped around her, cupping the tender flesh of her backside as his other hand slid between her legs. Breaking their kiss, he gazed at her with hooded eyes as his talented fingers found the sensitive spot under the hood of her sex. Circling with firm pressure, he continued to love her as she writhed above him.

"Mav..." she cried, closing her eyes as pleasure over-whelmed her. "Oh, *god...yes...*"

"Fuck, you're perfect like this. So tight and hot when you take me deep..." he rasped, his cock throbbing inside her.

The words sent shockwaves of heat through her body, causing her cells to ignite as she increased the pace of her hips. Tossing back her head, she closed her eyes, allowing herself to fall. Succumbing to his firm strokes on her clit as he claimed her, she launched into the climax, groaning with pleasure as he moaned below her.

Her inner walls milked him as he shouted her name. Clenching her ass in his broad hands, he anchored her, pumping inside her with furious strokes before his body stiffened and he joined her in the abyss. Jets of release coated her core as she collapsed against him, craving him upon every inch of her skin. His body convulsed in tiny bursts before he hummed in approval against her neck.

"Damn, babe, that was good." Nuzzling her neck, he encircled her with his arms as she burrowed against him.

"We have a lot of sex to make up for," she teased, running her nails over his chest. He shivered beneath her before nipping her earlobe.

"That we do. We'll fit that in between bouts of you working to save the world. I mean, go big or go home, right?"

Snickering, she nodded. "Truth." Resting her chin on her hand, her thoughts drifted to her sister. "I can't believe Raquel betrayed us. Geezus, Mav. I never saw it coming."

"Do you think you can forgive her?"

Sighing, she shrugged. "I don't know. I'm pissed as hell. But no matter how angry I am, we have to save her. Once she's safe with us, we can figure out the rest."

Maverick nodded as he caressed her.

"Arianna will feel the same. She'll want atonement, but she'll want to save Raquel first. Better to be punished by your family than your enemies."

"I imagine her first goal will be helping Dominic regain his strength," Maverick said. "Now that we know he's going to make it, we can help rehabilitate him while you work in the lab. We need him strong."

"Thank god he survived. He's healthy and his prognosis is good. I think he can regain his strength over the course of a few weeks if he's willing to train with you."

"He will. The man's a stubborn SOB, and Arianna will push him. He needs that."

"They need each other," Dani said softly, aching for her sister to find the love she deserved. "Who better to tear down walls than someone who erected ones just as thick?"

"There's my optimist," he teased, chucking her nose.

"I just want her to be happy," she whispered, pressing her cheek to his chest. "They both deserve that."

Feeling her lids grow heavy, Dani relaxed into her husband's body, soothed by his soft strokes against her skin. Although the tomorrows were unknown, Dani reveled in the knowledge Maverick would be by her side for the journey. His strength was her guidepost; his love, her unwavering reminder she still was deserving, even after the pain she'd involuntarily unleashed.

Dwelling on the destruction wouldn't bring her peace, but mending and repairing it might. Resolved, she vowed to do her best to save the world she'd inadvertently destroyed, one tomorrow at a time.

Before You Go

Thank you for starting this new journey with me! As much as I LOVE writing my Etherya's Earth books, I need to keep things fresh and pepper in new stories with different elements from time to time. I hope you loved Dani and Maverick as much as I did.

Ready to see what happens between Arianna and Dominic? You can find out in **Scorched Redemption**, Book 2 of the Sendaxa Chronicles trilogy!

You can browse all my books at RebeccaHefnerBooks.com!

Wishing you lots of happy reading and thank you for supporting indie authors! - *Rebecca*

ALSO BY REBECCA HEFNER

The Sendaxa Chronicles
Book 1: Repressed Echoes
Book 2: Scorched Redemption
Book 3: Fated Salvation

Etherya's Earth Series
Prequel: The Dawn of Peace
Book 1: The End of Hatred
Book 2: The Elusive Sun
Book 3: The Darkness Within
Book 4: The Reluctant Savior
Book 4.5: Immortal Beginnings
Book 5: The Impassioned Choice
Book 5.5: Two Souls United
Book 6: The Cryptic Prophecy
Book 6.5: Garridan's Mate
Book 7: The Diplomatic Heir
Book 7.5: Sebastian's Fate
Book 8: The Solitary Protector

Prevent the Past Trilogy
Book 1: A Paradox of Fates
Book 2: A Destiny Reborn
Book 3: A Timeline Restored